A String of Beads
&
Other Stories

A Sheila-Na-Gig Anthology

Edited by John Bullock

Sheila-Na-Gig Editions
Russell, KY
Hayley Mitchell Haugen, Editor
www.sheilanagigblog.com

Contents

A String of Beads

During this month's weekend with her father, which her mother said might be her last, Nora had filled the black patent leather purse, a St. Monica's rummage sale find, with the shells she'd been told to abandon on the beach. The only other shells she'd ever seen were glued to the top of a cigar box at Granny's house, where the old woman kept decades-old Valentine's cards from Papaw Nick, who was not Granny's husband and never would be. When the girl asked why, her grandmother just said, "If it ain't broke, don't fix it."

The shells of her box were small peachy spirals that made it so nothing could be stacked on top of it. Whenever the girl wanted, she could go upstairs and take out all the cards with fat baby cupids and red hearts, spreading them across the white crocheted blanket, organizing them by year, then by amount of text, then by amount of sap and lovey gooey.

A card with a love sonnet and filigreed corners scored significantly higher than a naked baby saying, "Aiming at you," with a wink on its pudgy round face. She'd add up Papaw Nick's score and he always came out ahead of Mariner, Granny's first and only husband, from whom there were no cards in the shell box.

Sometimes Granny would walk in on her while she was sorting: "Put those old things up. You'll get dust all over everything."

"They're not dusty, that's just the box. I leave that on the shelf. See! See!"

"Put them up."

Nora would slowly scoop them from the bed, letting them land in whatever old order in the box.

The shells she'd found at Lake Erie might make for a good box; it'd look different from Granny's, but it would still be a good one. All the shells were gray and striped, looking like the slim older sisters of the clams she had seen in tanks at the grocery store. Her mother often hurried the cart past them, otherwise the girl would stop and once stopped would become transfixed by the lobsters in the next tank, their little pinchers in tight blue bands. Whereas some children might mourn the predicament of the lobsters in their gentle children's voices, Nora would raise her hands in makeshift pincers, looking at her mother with pleading eyes and a rolled out bottom lip: "Please don't eat me, please." She'd mime great strength trying to move her thumb and forefinger apart. "No danger there, you're fourteen bucks a pound, buddy," her mother would say. It was much faster to roll quickly on and circumvent the theatrics of it all.

Her father had said to leave the shells on the rocky beach, but he hadn't said why, so Nora was inclined to pay him no mind. They were closed up tight. Maybe they had pearls. She wasn't sure if mussels made pearls or if that was something only oysters did. She was anxious to find out. She could use the shells to decorate a box for all the love letters she hadn't gotten yet and the pearls to make a bracelet to replace the one of Granny's she'd broken. It had been pink and delicate and probably not real pearls.

She'd admired it every time she'd opened the lid of the jewelry box on top of Granny's dresser. The box was so full it barely closed, though she'd never seen her wear anything except a red Minford Falcons button, and even that only on Friday nights when the whole family would load up in her father's van to go watch her cousin Tater play ball out at the stadium. Each piece in the box seemed to have its own life.

"Who gave you this one?" She'd hold up a heavy turquoise in the shape of the sun.

"Your uncle George bought me that on the trip out West."

"What about this one?" A feather of sparkly pink glass with a rusty brooch pin.

"Your father brought that back for me his first Christmas off to school. We were all real proud of him then."

"Not now?"

"What else is in there?" Granny rummaged among the costume jewelry and wooden crosses. "Now here's a pretty thing."

"That's my favorite!" The pink pearls were all the same diameter and smooth as smooth could be, except where the paint was flaking away and showing a glimpse of the white plastic underneath.

"These were from Willis, my first boyfriend."

"You had boyfriends?" Someday she assumed she too would have at least one, but for now boyfriends were something only women on TikTok and her mother had. She couldn't imagine that word meaning anything other than men in denim jackets who smelled of diesel, Marlboros, and energy drinks. They all looked like shorter/taller/fatter/thinner versions of her father. Boyfriend meant "almost but not quite." She sometimes worried how many almosts she'd have to try. The process seemed tiring and not particularly advantageous, except for the last guy who always brought her mother a box of clementines when he'd run routes to the South. She liked the little almost-what-an-orange-should-be. This was the only time "almost but not quite" seemed worth the hassle.

"Of course I had boyfriends." Granny stalled a moment. "Well, two at least. There was Willis then there was Mariner. I guess three, there's Nick now I suppose."

"Mariner was your boyfriend?"

"That's often how it goes, yes."

Nora pondered this for a bit. As far as she could remember, her father had been her mother's husband first and then sometimes her boyfriend, but more often than not he was just "your father." She couldn't imagine him with a Marlboro hanging from his lower lip. From what she'd seen, boyfriends smoke, husbands don't.

"Is there anything in here from him?"

"Who?"

"Mariner, is there anything from Mariner?"

"Just this." She held up a gold brooch with a purple heart in the middle and in the middle of the heart a wigged man in profile.

"Can I wear it?"

"No, you may not."

"What about the bracelet?"

"Take good care of it?"

"Of course."

"Just to Margie's shower then. Take it right off when you get back."

Her cousin Margie was getting married and everyone was dressing up for the bridal shower. Margie worked at Dr. Abramson's office on the West Side, which meant all her work friends would wear tight jeans and bring fancy presents in large silver bags with tissue paper on top. Nora had been excited to wear the pearls on her wrist, thinking that perhaps someone might mistake her for one of the nurses from Margie's work. She was big for ten and certain she could pass for at least eighteen, if not twenty.

While the adults had played games and drank punch from small glasses, Nora had run her finger back and forth along the pearls at her wrist. A boyfriend? Granny had had a boyfriend?

"Leave off those now, you don't want to break it," Aunt Shelia said as she passed on her way to the kitchen for more of the white meltaway mints.

It wasn't four seconds later when Nora heard the first of the beads hit the floor. Not a slow to fast progressive spill like she'd seen on sitcoms, but a furious dumping of everything at once. Instead of picking them up, she cried. Granny gathered the remnants up for her.

"It's okay, sometimes the strings wear out. Nothing to worry about. I didn't really care for them much anymore anyway."

"Pass 'em here and I'll take them to the trash for you." Margie held a cupped hand out toward Granny.

"No, no, that's okay. I'll just pitch them when I get home." Granny scooped each bead carefully from the floor and placed them in the small zipper part of her purse where the Doublemint and Juicy Fruit lived. No one questioned her and the evening went on with the games and Sprite punch and gossipy whispers Nora had come to expect from her father's family.

The girl knew she could replace the bracelet if only these mussels had pearls in them. When her father had seen her struggling with the weight of the bag, she told him it was full of rocks from the shore, that she had a new fish tank at her mother's and wanted to make them feel welcome, doll up the place a bit.

"Okay," he'd said, "you'd just better not have any of those mussels in there. They're those endangered ones."

She assured him she did not.

"Where did you guys go this weekend? Everything smells gross and there's mud all over your shoes," her mother said when she got home that evening.

"Up to the lake."

Her mother said nothing. It was farther away than she'd have preferred but still within the custody arrangement. It wasn't worth making a fuss.

"What's in the bag?" Her mother had noticed the weight.

"Just rocks for the fish."

"What fish?"

"The ones you're buying me when you get off work tomorrow." It seemed as good a time as any to make her pitch.

"If memory serves me right, I already said no to that."

"Oh? Did you?"

Her mother rolled her eyes and handed her back the bag.

"Get your stuff unpacked, I need to start up laundry soon or my jeans won't have time to dry before work tomorrow."

The bag was now hanging from the doorknob in her room. Nora wondered what she'd do if only one mussel had a pearl inside. It wouldn't be enough to make a whole new bracelet. Granny deserved a whole new bracelet, the best in the world. Nora had watched her carefully put the beads into a Ziploc bag and then the bag in her jewelry box when they got back from the shower. If she could get a new bracelet made for her before next month's visit she'd save the old woman the work of putting it back together. She knew she had until at least next month because when she'd asked her granny when she planned on fixing it, she said "eventually" and left it at that, which meant that repairing the bracelet would be like so many other things around Granny's. The broken railing on the back porch or the weakening floorboards in the bathroom that would all get fixed "when they get fixed" or "when someone gets around to it." Which, Nora was coming to realize, meant something closer to later than sooner and maybe even never.

"Why don't you ask Dad to fix it?" Nora had suggested once about the porch railing.

"Wouldn't want to get in the way of his sitting around."

This answer seemed fair to the girl. Her father did spend a decent amount of time sitting in front of his computer building houses and farms out of blocks that looked vaguely like what they were supposed to be.

"Use your imagination, kid," her father had told her when she complained that his game seemed boring. "You can't just focus on what it looks like now, you have to think about what it might look like someday when you've got it all finished." He'd shown her a completed town the server admin had built. It had a castle and pens full of animals and even a whale-shaped thing in a tank full of what Nora assumed was water. Everything still just looked like colored blocks on a screen. When Nora grew bored of watching her father play his game, she would give up and scroll through TikToks on her phone. It was only supposed to be for emergencies, and Nora had felt that her head exploding from boredom certainly qualified.

Her mother disagreed. When the cell bill came that month, she hit the roof at the data charges the girl had racked up while at her dad's.

"You can't pull yourself away from that shit for one weekend a month?" Nora heard her mother yelling on the phone. "Get it together, Ryan."

Her father's response was too soft for her to hear, but whatever it was made her mother's jaw tighten.

"Oh, really? Well, I think you don't deserve to see her if that's all you can manage to do with her. And I'm pretty sure a judge would agree with me."

The only thing Nora heard clearly in her father's garbled response was "know my rights."

"We'll see."

She knew that when her mother used that tone of voice that nothing good would come of it for the person on the other end.

It wasn't long after that that her dad started taking her places on his weekends. They'd gone to a Con at a hotel downtown and a Renaissance Faire about two hours away. Her father liked things where people were dressed up and acting like something other than what they were. Nora could see where this would be appealing to him since she'd heard her mother tell a boyfriend once that Nora's dad was a loser not living up to his potential. Why look for a better job when you could already be a Starfleet captain or a Renaissance knight? She understood all this more than the video game and enjoyed watching people in ill-designed costumes trying to go about their day without straining or ripping their outfits.

There were also a lot of kids her own age or a little older running around, especially at the Con. She'd followed a girl dressed as Mildred Hubble from the Worst Witch for a bit without getting up the nerve to talk to her. Then she'd eavesdropped on two boys in the Snack Café who she guessed were around fourteen, practically adults.

The boys were dressed as someone she didn't recognize, in slim -fitting suits with one wide lapel. They were talking about some new anime. She didn't watch much anime, so it might have been old, she wasn't sure, but she'd never heard of it. She imagined herself brave; she imagined herself walking over to them and sitting down, asking them questions about the shows they watch and the things they do. She saw herself as sparkling, charming, a real catch.

When she'd stand up to move toward them, something would pull her back down to her seat. Up, down, half a dozen times until a woman in a green Star Fleet uniform who may have been an actress that sometimes had a cult following and sometimes didn't, or may have been just somebody's mom, came over, put her hand on Nora's shoulder and said, "Easy there, you'll wear a groove in the floor, kid," before walking on to either a meet and greet line of fans or to go to the bathroom. Nora was unsure which since both kinds of lines looked fairly similar. Eventually she tired of her own cowardice and indecision and went looking for her father. She found him coming out of a panel on cartoons of the 80s. He looked happier than she'd ever seen him as he chatted rapidly with a woman dressed as a Minecraft Creeper.

"Jesus, Ryan, take her someplace real for once. This is your last chance, I swear," her mother had yelled into the phone as she helped Nora unload her suitcase the Sunday she'd come back from the Con.

"Your case would be weak sauce and you know it. She's not in any danger, she's just bored," she heard her father say.

She was pretty sure this is how they'd ended up at Lake Erie the day after Margie's shower. They'd left early and the drive had been long, four hours at least. Nora had tried to talk to her dad a few times on the way up, but he seemed hidden in his own head, so eventually she just read some Percy Jackson and tried to convince her brain that she wasn't bothered by the fact that her father didn't want to talk to her.

"What's the plan?" she asked when they finally arrived in the parking lot of Headlands Beach State Park, which her father had chosen despite the Trip Advisor reviews warning that it was "dirty, rocky, and uncomfortable."

"What?"

"The plan. What's the plan? What are we doing? Boating? Fishing? Swimming? Well, I didn't bring a suit, so no swimming I guess."

"Don't have much of one, just figured we'd see what happens."

Nora was irked by her father's lack of forethought. He'd made a two-page itinerary for the Con and highlighted hot spots on his map of the Ren Faire. He had at least thirteen different files on his computer with notes and plans for the replica of Tracey Park he was going to make someday in Minecraft, once he finished his build of the peninsula out at Roosevelt Lake. She knew the lake was where her parents had been married, but she didn't know much about the park. Their first date maybe? When she'd asked, her father had given a dreamy and mischievous smile: "Nothing you need to know about, kid." But he'd driven her four hours with no plan?

"Why'd we come up here then? We could have hung out at Granny's with no plan and saved the gas." Nora was hyperaware of the cost of gas since it was her mother's favorite excuse for not taking her to the zoo up in Columbus.

"Gets your mom off my back at least. She wants real, I'll show you real."

Nora sighed in the way only a ten-year-old can, full of judgement and ennui. Though really, anyone can sigh that way, it's just that before ten you don't need to and after ten you know better and just sigh silently to yourself. She shut the car door and headed for the shore to see what there was to see. Her father trailed after her, swatting at the stable flies clouding around his head while picking his way around wads of fresh gum melting on the hot asphalt of the parking lot.

He caught up with her when she stopped to poke at some partially exposed mussel shells clinging to large rocks at the waterline. She'd found a reasonably solid stick and was jabbing it first where the mussels had attached themselves to the rock and then between the shells.

"Hey . . . hey! Yo . . . yo! Cut that out," he said running up to her and grabbing the stick away. "What do you think you're doing?"

"Just seeing what happens. Maybe I can find some pearls in them and make a new bracelet for Granny. Or maybe there's enough to make one for her and one for me," she finished dreamily.

"Not likely." He threw the stick on the ground and started walking down the shore. Nora wasn't sure if she was meant to follow or stay put, so she stayed put. Eventually she pried a few mussels from their home and stashed them in the small black handbag she'd picked up the day before at a church rummage sale. Eventually her father came back, and they got in the car to go home. On the way home Nora had tried to ask her dad about Mariner since he was still on her mind from the day before.

"Don't know much about him, died when I was five." And that was that.

Four hours there and four hours back at a lake that didn't feel all that different from parts of Lake Roosevelt back home. A little bigger, a little grayer, a little rockier, but all in all the same.

By the time Nora's mother had gone to bed it was late, but the girl had fought sleep so she could check on her mussels. She couldn't figure out a way to get them open to check them for pearls. She cracked the bag a bit in the dark stillness of the house and was horrified by what she saw. Ten shells open, ten living things drying out over two hundred miles from home. The insides of the shells were shiny and looked like pearls, but there wasn't an actual pearl in sight, just a dying gray muck and the smell of rot and lake water.

Her heart raced and she searched her mind for a solution. Her father had told her not to take them; she couldn't call him for help without an angry lecture that would be worse even than the time she'd told her uncle Rick where her father's Notch Apple was hidden in his game. She hadn't meant to be ornery that time, really she hadn't. She'd been watching Rick play at Granny's one day and it'd just come up. Her uncle was way more interesting to watch than her father. All her father did was build things, and usually they were only places around town she could just go to in real life if she wanted to. But Rick stole gear from other people's houses, went looking for zombies and spiders to fight (instead of only fighting when they showed up at this house like her father did), and sometimes he'd even burn things when the builder wasn't online.

He'd been rummaging around some stranger's Hogwart's Great Hall looking for chests to raid. "Hmm . . . where would I hide the good shit? Where . . . would . . . I . . . hide the good shit?" His talking slowed but didn't stop as he clicked his way around the hall.

"My dad hides stuff behind lava."

"He does, does he? Like what kind of stuff?"

"Like that apple he used to have framed on his wall. The one he was talking about at Easter dinner."

"Ah . . . let's see . . . Ender Pearls . . . 16 . . . good, good. Thank you very much, my little friend."

Nora watched him go to her father's basement and found a lava flow surrounded by stone blocks (in the game; in real life her father lived in a one-bedroom apartment with a dripping bathroom tap). He threw the pearl through the lava and came out in a small room full of chests.

"Tele . . . ported!" he said, triumphantly.

Her father was so mad at her when really he should have been mad at Rick, or really-really, when you got deep down to it, with himself for not protecting what he had better.

Her mother thought the bag was full of rocks. And if she didn't want a tank of goldfish and tetras around she certainly wasn't going to be thrilled with a bag of stinky mussels with no pearls. Nora had no choice but to take care of it herself. And she did it the only way she could think of. She snuck through the hallway to the kitchen, unlatched the sliding door, stepped out into the cool of the August night, and flung the mussels into the yard. Most landed silently in the grass, but one struck the lid of their grill first, making a loud chunk she was sure could be heard throughout the quiet neighborhood. The grill hadn't been used since her father had moved out, and the hit shook a little rust free. She felt a heaviness in her heart but could not tell if it was for the lost lives of the mussels or the lost pearls and the bracelet she'd never make for Granny.

In the morning, she could hear her mother yelling on the phone.

"Well, I don't know, Ryan, but she did, I watched her do it." Nora had forgotten what a light sleeper her mother was and how loud the latch on the old sliding door was as well.

"No, *you* need to talk to her about this. Take some fucking responsibility for once." This seemed unfair since Nora felt she deserved some credit for being extra sneaky in getting the mussels past her dad. It wasn't his fault she was a super genius.

Nora's mother did not mention the mussels, which wasn't surprising. Neither did her father, which also was not surprising given his track record with both disciplinary action and just interaction with the girl in general. Nora thought she had gotten off scot-free, until Friday, when a package came for her. It was from Granny. Though this particular package was unexpected, it wasn't unusual for Granny to send her little things every now and then even though she only lived across town. In the box was a small bracelet of the most beautiful green glass beads Nora had ever seen. They were clean and new, and the box they came in smelled of perfumed department store air. With them came a note in Granny's overly round and hard to decipher cursive script:

> Nora,
> I appreciate the thought, but have some sense, kid. I can take care of myself. Here's a trinket of your own, you don't need no boys anyway.
>
> Love,
> Granny

The girl put the bracelet on her wrist and held it up to the light, admiring the way the surface of the beads sparkled like the real emeralds she'd seen on television. They were perfect, just perfect.

Sarah Kontopoulos

Happiness on the Beach

After we lost Audrey, the family was never the same. We shattered like granite, irreparably split along a vein; you could fit the jagged pieces back into place, but they would not hold, ever again.

Mother blamed herself, as did everyone else of course, whether they told her to her face or not. If only Mother had intercepted. Audrey might have been spared. If only she had been closer to Audrey, or watched her more closely, or fed her different food, or, or, or.

Little Audrey with her flaxen braids and two missing front teeth. Who loved to dress like Mother in a mini version of whatever green dress, tasseled shorts, or overalls Mother wore.

Mother said she shouldn't have looked away, even for a minute, and she repeated this in myriad ways over the days and months after Audrey was lost. She said a mother's first obligation was to protect her children from the world, other people, fluke accidents, even from herself.

We tried to tell her, "It was an accident, Mother! No one could have saved Audrey."

But she wouldn't listen.

The police declared the incident unavoidable.

It didn't matter. Mother couldn't hear it. She would never let herself forget.

We were only halfway through our family vacation when it happened, so we stayed an extra week while Mother and Dad dealt with the aftermath. They handled the details so capably, contacting the authorities and family back home, deftly moving us from our grand rented vacation villa to two rooms in a cramped, old beach hotel in Platanias that was cheaper and "good enough."

Happiness on the Beach sat three stories high at the western end of a long string of hotels and resorts on the beachfront strip. It was covered in bright orange stucco with Mediterranean blue balconies. The rows of rooms were studded with oversized, incompetent air conditioners jutting as far outside the window as they did inside the rooms, never quite reaching a comfortable coolness.

Us children—me, Greg, and Theresa—shared a single room with two beds and were left to make sense of the abrupt transformation of our family life.

From the glittering hotness of beach days and orange grove tours, of eating late dinners under olive and mulberry trees, serenaded by cicadas, where our parents clinked together tiny glasses of raki, smiling "Yammas" to each other, and where we later tumbled into cool beds and were rocked to sleep by the lovely drafts of early June, to sweating alone in our hotel room all day in the late June heat that had crept up on us, watching Greek TV or ancient American shows like "Bonanza" and "The Monkees," ordering tepid yogurt and pita bread from the humid downstairs taverna.

The beach only yards away but forbidden while our parents were out handling the adult details of losing a child. Every afternoon they returned and took us on our only foray of the day to the same taverna. We ate a quick and nearly silent dinner of dakos, and dry souvlaki with fries, and trudged back upstairs to climb back into our stale beds.

When it was time to fly home to Michigan, Mother was anxious and inconsolable. She wanted to stay close to where Audrey had last been seen.

It took all of us, and multiple little pills from Dad—Xanax, I later learned—to convince her it was time to go.

"We have nowhere to stay, Mother!"

"Don't you want to sleep in your own cool bed?"

"Audrey would want us to go home."

We naively hoped it would be enough to convince her.

On the flight home we dozed at a tolerable temperature for the first time in almost two weeks. And I remember the deep relief when finally, after customs, the baggage claim, and a sad, silent drive we reached home.

I ran to my bedroom and hugged my stuffed narwhal, Ninjacat.

Audrey and I shared a bedroom and I shut my eyes tightly against guilty thoughts about how it would all be mine now. No doubt Greg and Theresa did something similar. We all emerged an hour later stumbling downstairs, blurry eyed and hungry, to find our parents.

That was the moment my life divided resolutely into clear "before" and "after" memories.

Before, when we all convened downstairs around dinner time, Mother waited in the kitchen with a meal ready and the table laid. Dad hovered nearby, and we would gather at the kitchen table to eat and talk about our day.

After, starting with that first meal home after our plane ride, we rarely ate meals together. We kids wanted to believe the bad dream was over, that our life would go back to how it had been. With Mother ready in the kitchen when we were hungry.

Instead, when we came downstairs for that first dinner, it was Dad we found. Shirtless in terry towel shorts, he fried something—it turned out to be scrambled eggs—at the stove. Bread browned in the toaster, and he had left a cutlery pile on the table to fend for itself. Mother wasn't there. But a glimpse through the open sliding door to the backyard revealed her barefoot staring into the woods behind our house.

"Mother?"

She heard me but didn't answer.

That scene became our routine. I learned not to expect much from Mother anymore: not waking me up for school, not smiling, not washing my clothes, not cooking, not hugging, nor taking us to the dentist.

Sometimes she came through and performed stonily, but often she didn't. The only thing we could rely on was the inconsistent probability of either.

Dad was ever reactive and would only jump in and rescue us with a lift to the appointment when the dentist, doctor, or teacher failed to coordinate with Mother and called him in desperation.

In those times, we knew Mother would stay unreliable for the next day or two. That if we wanted her, she would be in the back garden, barefoot and silent, staring into the abyss.

"When will she get better?" I whispered to Dad, making sure Mother couldn't hear me through the screen door.

"Doesn't she love us anymore?"

"Of course she does. She's just so upset about losing Audrey. Sometimes her guilt overwhelms her. Try to understand."

We children would look at each other with a wide-eyed need for affirmation. It wasn't fair! We were still alive! Mother should care about us more than Audrey!

And, of course, she did, we thought we knew. It was just that her grief could not be overridden.

We agreed to try to understand. To hope against hope that Mother would come back to us. That she would lay to rest her grief and guilt. That she would find a way to heal. And forget Audrey so our family could be first in her heart again.

Theresa was the first one to realize Mother was gone.

It was a Tuesday and I'd just been delivered by my best friend's mother after soccer practice. Theresa answered the door in a panic: "Mother's gone. We can't find her!"

We ran into the house and found Dad and Greg discussing who had seen her last—Dad, that morning—and where she might have gone.

Hours later, after Dad looked for our passports and checked his credit card transactions, he discovered the plane tickets to Frankfurt and Crete.

Mother had booked the flights the previous week—on my 11th birthday. We'd had a family party to celebrate. That weekend I'd had a pool party with my three best friends and one of them had slept over.

Unlike previous years where Mother planned everything in detail, Dad hastily planned both celebrations two days before. There were no paper plates and coordinating cups with "Happy Birthday!" on them. But when Dad realized Mother would not come through for my birthday, he scrambled to.

Despite all that was different, the day was happy, I thought. Everyone seemed so joyful and content, and it was a great relief to celebrate anything. I felt hopeful again for a new kind of normal, where we looked forward to birthdays and fun, even if Audrey didn't exist anymore.

And then, Mother flew back to Crete, and it all fell apart again. She didn't respond when Dad tried to call. There were more credit transactions over the days following. Mostly for food and for Happiness on the Beach, where Mother had apparently returned.

Dad finally reached her for a hasty conversation before she hung up.

She said that Happiness was where she felt closest to Audrey, and it was the beach at the hotel that was on her mind most when she stood in the backyard.

Mother planned to stay in Crete, on the beach in Platanias, and wait until Audrey came back; not if, but when.

The implausibility of Mother's plan was obvious to everyone, and we wondered how she didn't know it too. She couldn't stay in Platanias; Audrey was never coming back. And she had the other three of us to live for—four, with Dad.

Dad reached Mother on the phone again the next week. Afterward, he calmly told us everything. Mother was working as a maid at Happiness to pay for her room. She had no plan to come back to Michigan anytime soon. There were no kisses or love sent.

I was bewildered and untethered at Mother's going away; a half-collapsed helium balloon of unpredictable feelings, rising and drifting with the breeze. Fear, anxiety, and a howling loneliness filled and overpowered me.

Lying in bed at night, in our room, my heart pounded, and my eyes poured while Audrey's taped-up school drawings looked on with an occasional flutter.

"Imagine how Audrey feels," I consoled myself.

Not long after, my emotions abruptly stopped and were replaced by emptiness as numb as wood.

I couldn't feel anything then, even if I wanted to. I didn't know what to call this or how it had happened until I was much older and learned about disassociation. My feelings were too muddled and too much, and so my mind had simply unplugged from them.

The others dealt with theirs in different ways: Greg cycled between silent anger and explosions, and Theresa surprised us all by becoming Mother's most vocal supporter, rationalizing why she had to go away.

Grandma Jean, Mother's mother, moved in with us to help. Jean was 85 and needed our help as much as we hers. She relied on Mother too and hadn't predicted her only daughter would run away to Crete.

Jean brought with her an oversized suitcase made of thick beige twill and scented like musty books. Stuffed inside was her collection of zippered robes in tasteful prints and muted pastels. It was her uniform most days. Grandma Jean liked to stew prunes, and their cloying sweetness perfumed the kitchen and her robes. She was great at crossword puzzles, and after a time there was a trail of them through the house.

Looking back, I wondered if it was a wonderful, or terrible, way for her to spend the last years of her life. Grandma Jean never expected to step into Mother's shoes, and how could she at that age? At best she was a comforting companion who could order food or call the police if anything disastrous happened. But otherwise, we were on our own.

Audrey had been around most of my life and I felt uneasy as the youngest. No one talked about the disorientation of losing your sister and your mother. We just got on with each day, surviving the moments until bedtime.

"There, there, dear," Grandma Jean would say when lostness and sadness must have shown on my face.

She paired, "Don't let it get you down," with vague pats on my hand or shoulder. It was a comfort.

Dad hired a housekeeper to clean and cook for us once a month. It was all he could afford but never enough to keep up with five people, three of them teenagers. The house was in a constant state of chaos and disarray. Jean couldn't match the demands of our laundry, belongings, and activities. Still, we needed her in a way she hadn't been needed in a long time and that was something.

We reached Mother periodically on the phone. She talked mostly about the weather, with the conversation hovering around how hot Crete was, and the last time there had been rain.

In winter we heard how there was snow in the White Mountains. We knew nothing else about her life there.

"When are you coming back, Mother?" We asked. Silence, and then a change of topic, usually to food.

* * *

With all this, life had settled into a certain rhythm by the year I turned twelve. I'd learned to lie and tell friends and their parents that my mom was away a lot "visiting sick relatives."

Then Theresa turned eighteen and made an unexpected announcement. Four of us lingered over the remnants of Jean's Tuesday Rice-A-Roni and rotisserie chicken dinner. Greg was at swim practice and would eat later, alone. A lazy fly buzzed inside a column of air just inside the open sliding glass door.

Theresa said that she had saved her money and was going to visit Mother in Crete. Her mind was made up and she had a ticket for the week after graduation.

We stared at her in silence.

I was caught off guard and felt my bearings slipping again. It hadn't occurred to me that any of us could go there. Only that Mother could come home but wouldn't. Why hadn't we tried?

When Theresa first called home, her voice was full of excitement about Crete and Mother. They spent a morning at Stavros Beach where *Zorba the Greek* was filmed; the saganaki was just like she remembered it, etc.

By this time Mother had a work visa, had learned some Greek, and was working in a travel agent's office as an assistant. She had a small apartment not far from Happiness and still worked and ate there occasionally.

After a couple of weeks, something changed when we talked to Theresa. Her voice took on an earnestness about Mother's plan to find Audrey.

I couldn't decide what made less sense: that Mother thought she could find Audrey, or that Theresa bought into the idea too.

Then Dad couldn't reach her until the day after she was supposed to fly home. He had waited at airport arrivals for an hour before leaving. Theresa had decided to stay in Crete a little longer. A student visa meant she could study at the technical college there.

She never came home again.

And then it was just Dad, Greg, Jean, and I left to knock around the house. Dad never remarried, and we lived together as a loose collective. Years passed this way. Greg graduated high school and left for college, and Jean passed away. We buried her in a favorite zippered robe and, at her memorial, recounted fond stories about her hearty cooking. Mother and Theresa did not return for any of it.

When I graduated from high school there were just the three of us to celebrate. My helium balloon careened again. How different life would look if we still had Audrey, Mother, and Theresa.

I was twenty-six the September I made my way to Crete. Lord knows why I wanted to go. It was sixteen years after Audrey. I spoke with Mother and Theresa rarely, and only when I called them. Perhaps two or three times a year. Every Christmas they sent a generic postcard of the Chania lighthouse.

That winter I was getting married in Michigan and I wanted to see them. There were a few relatives from my side coming to the wedding. And I didn't have the courage to invite Mother and Theresa. What would be worse, facing their silence or the possibility that they might actually attend? Nothing had ever come of their search for Audrey because, well, of course it couldn't.

At Chania airport I sweated an hour in the shade for my rental car. Somehow, they charged me $100 more than what I had paid for it online. I'd been warned about the price gouging of tourists but didn't argue. A printed sign taped roughly to the back wall read, "Tipping is not just a city in China."

I typed an address into my GPS and twenty-five minutes later parked in front of the travel agency where Mother still worked. She was a full agent now. The agency was inside a street-level storefront with floor-to-ceiling windows, so from the street you could see everything happening inside.

A large main room with three desks, and a "private" office also enclosed in glass made up the visible spaces. Sensibly, the bathroom was enclosed in drywall.

Mother sat inside the first room at a heavy wooden desk.

Her hair was cut into a shoulder-length bob and had gone a dark silver. She wore a headset and microphone, and she gestured while speaking to someone on the phone.

Facing her at a similar desk from across the midsized room was a woman with cheap-looking bleached hair, who wore large turquoise earrings and a matching oversized necklace.

To anyone else walking by the scene looked normal.

But for me it brought up all the old questions: Why had Mother left us? What had I done wrong? Where was Theresa?

I called the travel agency from my cell and Mother answered the phone. "Yassas, XX travel agency."

"Oh, hello, I'm calling about your day trip to Balos Island?" I didn't alter my voice.

Mother's voice was professional but flat and she didn't recognize mine. I watched her through the window while we chatted. Did she never think about me?

"Oh yes, let me put you through to my daughter Audrey, she can help you."

My mouth gaped and cement seemed to fill my stomach. I was glad then that I had called from the car first.

Her daughter? Audrey?

Mother pressed a button and music started playing on my end. I watched incredulously as she called out to the bleached blond who nodded and donned her own headset.

"Hello? This is Audrey," Theresa said. "I understand you're interested in our private boat trip to Balos?"

Theresa was Audrey now? I struggled to make my mind catch up.

"Uh, yes, yes, I'd like to know what, what, uh, what days you're free this week." I stumbled, hoping she wouldn't hear the waver in my voice, and then added, "And what is the least expensive day?"

"Oh, we have several times available," Theresa-Audrey started. "You're a single, yes? Well, you could join another group and pay half price."

We went on this way for a few minutes. She gave me pricing and information that weren't available online before I thanked her and said I would call back.

All I could think about was the summers we—Theresa and I— had jumped together at our town's summer festival. Our long hair rising and falling as we giggled and bounced inside the blue, green, and yellow inflatable castles. Theresa's voice still had the same lilt. I missed her.

After the call, I drove around Platanias for a while with the cool air from the car's AC to help me think. It was still very hot at a time when most people would not go out for hours. I checked into Happiness on the Beach at 8pm and asked for the room we kids had shared after Audrey was gone. Now the Happiness was orange with yellow balconies. The ACs were newer and quieter but everything else was the same. I marveled that the three of us had stayed so obediently in our room while Mother and Dad were out.

For the next two days, I drove to different beaches in the morning—what was the point of having a car if I didn't use it?—and spent afternoons on the beach under an umbrella in front of Happiness. I ate dinner in the taverna downstairs and waited. On the second night, Mother and Theresa-Audrey came in.

They were hard to miss, dressed alike in white kaftans with orange and pink swirls and a pair of sort-of high-heel sandals—espadrilles, I think. The only difference between them was that Theresa-Audrey wore the same turquoise jewelry set I had seen before.

Sourness filled my mouth. I might vomit. It was so strange to see them like this. Audrey had always liked to dress like Mother. But Theresa never had. Their twinning completed her transformation.

The two sat at a table across from mine and took their time ordering from the menu. Theresa-Audrey nattered away to Mother who was silent and blank, with the occasional nod. Theresa-Audrey seemed impervious to her quiet. I had my cell out and pretended to look at it whenever they looked my way, which wasn't often.

Were they happy?

Could they be, in this limbo life? I couldn't tell.

Theresa-Audrey seemed like she was, but maybe she was just pretending like the way she pretended she was Audrey. After sixteen years of it, I guessed it wasn't really limbo anymore, just life. Maybe Theresa had changed her name. By now so much time had passed that no one here would be asking questions about their lives before they came to Crete.

I wanted to villainize them, to imagine them as a freakish conjoined mother and daughter who dressed alike and had the same boyfriend. And I knew it wasn't possible to form a complete picture without talking to them and entangling myself in their new story, whatever it was.

After dinner, over slow sips of raki, I gave myself the remaining three days to approach them. When they went out to the beach after dinner, I trailed them but couldn't approach. This repeated the next few times I saw them at Happiness or through the window at the travel agency. I couldn't bring myself to follow them home.

Finally, the morning before my flight I sat in front of the travel agency one last time. What did I need from them? Why was I even there?

I was starting to feel untethered again. I'd been adrift all these years, alone. And then I remembered Dad, Greg, and Jean. Not alone, but a family, with them. Our life had been disorganized, but I discovered later that we were a lot like the other families we knew. Our granite pieces hadn't just broken, they'd been pulverized to a fine dust. And though it wasn't possible to meld them back together, they had transformed into a tornado of sand that gathered together and danced through centrifugal force.

Mother and Audrey-Theresa were just rocks in an office. Strangers who were utterly disconnected from me. I didn't need to know more about them to know how I felt about losing them. And I didn't want to know more about their strange life to appreciate what was beautiful about mine. I drove away to the airport without ever going inside.

When my plane reached altitude, I put on a sleep mask and pushed in earplugs. As I dozed I saw Mother and Theresa-Audrey together on Stavros Beach at sunset, dancing arm in arm like Zorba the Greek: Theresa with her fake blond hair, and Mother with a softening of her deadened, stony face.

But that vision seemed too self-indulgent and saccharine. And as I drifted to sleep a truer vision came to me: Mother and new Audrey wearing matching peach nightdresses, on twin beds across a large bedroom from each other. Mother sitting up reading, and Audrey lying down and tucked in.

Audrey said, "Good night, Mother."

And then Mother said, "Good night, Audrey," and clicked off the light.

They were content together like this, in their disconnected way. And I would never need to be part of their strange life to know my own happiness ever again.

Ed Davis

Ceremony

So far Cassie's wedding is not anything like how I'd envisioned it: happy folks gathering beneath lush green canopy here in the Pine Forest, hawk soaring above, blessing my best friend and her chosen mate. So far it's been more "Bridge Over Troubled Water" than "All You Need is Love."

As the scheduled entertainment, I'm qualified to make such distinctions.

Maybe another song will help? But no one's paying much attention to an old barely-a-boomer chick like me strumming and singing beside the path where folks enter from two directions: up the long bank from Shawnee Springs Creek or down from the Horace Mann statue meadow, our temporary parking lot. I feel a hand on my shoulder, and when I turn, Cass looks totally stressed out.

"Oh, Kate! Mom finally made it, but she's not happy."

My best friend looks beautiful, a portrait of innocence in her white embroidered blouse and iridescent long green skirt. The silver and turquoise necklace I'd bought in New Mexico years ago is the perfect touch; I had no idea when I gifted her with it that she'd wear it on her Big Day. At thirty-seven, she doesn't look any older than the young single mom I'd taken under my wing nearly a decade ago at the high school where we teach. I'd chosen her to mentor on Day One. I knew she needed nurturing. I'd watched her daughter Madison grow up and babysat her often over the past nine years while my mentee shopped for a new husband, a lengthy enterprise that resulted in much disappointment.

Madison now stands, basket of pinecones on her arm, ready to spread joy at the drop of a rusty needle. Though she's twelve, I feel she's still years away from being a teenager, with her frilly pink canopy bed and Olympic athletes rather than pop stars on her wall. She beams whenever I catch her eye, making me, as always, feel guilty. She'd always wanted to adore her "Auntie Kate," but I found myself putting up, if not exactly a wall, then a chain-mail veil between us. I could read her a story from the rocking chair but never felt all that comfortable cuddling. Cass saw the distance I needed but never said a word about it, gushing with gratitude for the tiniest contribution I made to her little family. She knows her old friend has demons. Is there a forty-five-year-old alive who doesn't?

And now it's looking like my mentee is facing hers. Cass looks around to make sure she's not overheard by the woman whose mind control was almost total till she threw in her lot with me, the Bad Influence. At least she doesn't cover her mouth with her hand when she stage-whispers:

"Mom just told me she's not staying the night in the room I booked for her at Peregrine House. She's not even staying for the reception. She's driving back to Cleveland right after the ceremony."

Casting a glance behind her, she waves at the daughter she'd had with Wolf Kline, the tattoo artist who, according to Cassie, remains the greatest grievance her mom holds against her. I will her not to cry, not now, not ever, over the woman standing alone, chin held high, in her navy blue realtor's uniform more suited to a funeral than a wedding. I resist telling Cass she should give up trying to please a woman certain to hate everything about this "hippy wedding," as her daughter said she'd surely call it. Instead, I shrug.

"So Mom misses out. At least she came for the ceremony. Maybe she'll get something out of it."

Not likely, say Cassie's swollen eyes. At least she isn't wearing makeup that will run, the lack of it doubtless another grievance for Mom in her high heels and mortician's outfit, although the invitation had made perfectly clear the forest setting. Cassie doesn't look in the least convinced.

"But Maddy loves her grandma. Because her grandma has given her everything that she never gave me."

"Your daughter will enjoy today if you enjoy it, sweetie." I reach out and thumb away the tears before they fall. "Don't let her see she's hurt you. Show Greg and Maddy they're all the family you need."

"And you, dear Kate."

I'm touched when she places her hand on my fingers laced atop the guitar. Then she whispers, "You're more my mother than she is."

I'm speechless for a couple of moments before I finally manage to mutter, "Go mingle. It's your day."

Turning, she approaches her young colleagues, who stand awkwardly, looking lost among the over-fifties who constitute most of the dozen invitees.

I decide to ratchet things up and play "Diamond in the Rough," imitating Shawn Colvin's fast, choppy guitar licks, singing loud. I want everybody in the crowd to know this soon-to-be bride isn't taking any shit off any authorities. Cassie's fellow thirty-somethings nod along, while Greg's mom, grandma, and Aunt Imelda (on a walker and portable oxygen) loudly talk over me—no easy feat. They form a scrum in the middle of the "sanctuary" where an opening in the canopy lets the light pour in.

Cass's mom is her only relative in attendance besides Madison. Mom glares at me, scorching the air between us, before facing the white bower Greg constructed, with intertwining ivy, daisies, and roses. Greg and his brother shlepped it over in two pieces earlier this morning, and it looks right at home. Mom had wanted the wedding ("if you have to be married again") held at Holy Angels in Cleveland.

Cassie almost caved to her wishes before my intervention. I invited her over for margaritas, and we listened to Colvin, Nicks, DiFranco, and Rickie Lee, the musical equivalent of a NOW meeting. After Cass was good and buzzed, I'd asked her what she wanted. Tears pouring, she'd said a Pine Forest wedding. In the days afterward, whenever she wavered, I reminded her how passionate she'd been that night about being married in the same place where Greg proposed last fall. Ultimately, she'd held firm. The only incense Mom would sniff would be the sharp silver scent of pine.

The instant I finish "Diamond," Greg walks right over, wearing his tight-lipped almost-a-grimace grin.

"I'm damn glad you're here, Kate."

"Yeah?"

I like Greg because he's in love with my best friend and treats her right. Though I had my doubts about her dating an Air Force pilot, he turned out to be gentle, kind, and smart. Most important, he's never gotten between us.

"The music's great. I hope you don't mind keeping it up a little longer." He looks around, lowers his voice. "Father Lyons isn't here yet."

I couldn't believe they'd gotten a priest. (A concession to Cassie's mom, of course.) I'd recommended Dan Farley, Shawnee Springs' lovable red-faced mayor, who married almost everybody in town.

"I think Father must've gotten lost," he whispers.

"No way! He'd call, right?"

He shakes his head. "It was all so last minute. Cassie had the Methodist minister from town lined up, but he had to cancel yesterday due to a family emergency. I think she arranged it through Father's secretary. What if she forgot to tell him?"

I look over his shoulder at Mom the Mortician, who's growing unhappier by the moment. She stands alone, clutching her purse like someone's going to steal it. Or maybe it's a shield because she doesn't know anybody. In spite of myself, I empathize a little. But surely a businesswoman like herself knows how to mingle, right?

"Don't sweat it, Greg. You guys are getting married, if I have to do it."

When he smiles, his eye corners crinkle. He's indicated before, subtly so as not to upset his beloved, that he's my ally in Cassie's parental recovery.

"Let's hope it doesn't come to that." Then he hears himself. "No offense!"

"None taken. I'll keep the tunes coming for a little longer."

Raising his thumb in solidarity, he slips back beside his betrothed, who's now bouncing from foot to foot like she needs to pee. Much longer and we'll all be looking for some privacy in the understory.

Belting out Joni's "Chelsea Morning," I circle the sanctuary, guarding the perimeter like a Border Collie. Toward the rear of the clearing, I notice a lean-to almost hidden in the underbrush. I'm surprised until I remember that visitors often build structures here to amuse themselves, try to get in touch with their inner Indian or some-such. But they don't usually place stones together in a fire ring or leave a ratty looking sleeping bag sprawled on the ground to air out.

Holy shit. Somebody's sleeping out here!

How had we not noticed during the rehearsal? But we'd been in a rush to finish before it rained again. Well, if he (I detect masculine aura) just keeps quiet for another thirty minutes or so, all should be well. If some derelict interferes, he'll have to contend with me. I move closer to the assembly and strum the intro to "Part of the Plan." Dan Fogelberg's hymn to self-actualization goes by all too quickly, leaving me wondering what else to play for such a subdued crowd.

Then the sound starts.

At first, I think it's the trill of a wood thrush. But when the same three trembly, sustained notes repeat exactly, I realize it's the reedy tone of a flute, mingling the lilt of the thrush with an owl's midnight whoo. Everyone has stopped talking, glancing around nervously to see where the notes might be coming from.

Me, too, but whether due to the forest's odd acoustics or maybe magic, I can't tell. Strumming tentatively, I find that C, G and D fit, so I play louder, Cassie smiling at me gratefully (anything to buy a bit more time while we wait for Father). Folks seem to relax, probably thinking the main event's beginning. Even Mom is looking around expectantly, as if actually noticing she's outdoors and it's sort of okay.

I wish I was okay, but I feel weird as the woodwind solo time-machines me back a dozen years to Taos Bookshop on the same day I'd bought the turquoise necklace Cassie's wearing. In the back of the shop, I'd found R. Carlos Nakai's *Canyon Trilogy* CD, wiped off the dust, approached the guy at the front and asked him if it was any good. His eyes nailed me like a butterfly to a board. "If the earth sang, it would sound exactly like Carlos Nakai."

On that first road trip West, Aaron and I had discovered the little adobe church on the high road between Taos and Santa Fe on our road trip to California to see the redwoods. We'd never heard of the "Lourdes of the Southwest," where the healing dirt cured all ills, spiritual, material, and psychological.

That July day, after Aaron withdrew from the sweaty heat of the Santuario's candle-lit room containing the open pit, I rubbed dirt on my forehead, seat of the migraines I'd suffered the past couple of years. Then, half-ashamed, I followed my mate into the larger adjacent room containing discarded crutches and photo after photo alongside handwritten testimonials pilgrims had left behind.

Three days later, driving through the mountains on the way to Sequoia National Park, when I told my husband what I'd done, he laughed. The dry desert air, he'd said, or even breezes off the ocean, had sent my headaches into remission. "They'll come back once you're home."

But I'd remained migraine-free until school resumed in the fall. "Post hoc ergo propter hoc," my philosophy prof husband would've said, had I bothered to inform him. "'After this, therefore because of this.' Your migraines would've stopped, anyway. You were on vacation—no stress."

I knew better than to bring it up again. For the time being, though, the memory of healing dirt went into the mental file marked "Vacation," to be revisited at some later date.

Within a year, Aaron and I got our biggest wish, when I became pregnant. Surely no one enjoyed gestating a baby more than I did. But I was determined to keep teaching as long as I could, despite my husband's protests. And I did, until my water broke during a faculty meeting. Still, all went well until the birth itself. Aaron and I'd never even heard of cord prolapse. When the umbilical cord dropped out of my cervix and wrapped around my unborn daughter's throat, she suffered brain damage that killed her within twenty-four hours.

It destroyed us.

In the aftermath, at the peak of our misery during a terrible fight, the most rational man I'd ever met lost his mind. He'd begged me, he shouted, to quit working, rest, and prepare my body. I'd made a big mistake; it would've never happened if I'd listened to him. It was his grief speaking, but I had to protect my own heart or die. That was our last fight.

Then, sometime between Lucinda's funeral and my divorce, the Santuario returned to me in a dream. A river blue as the ocean's edge flowed at the bottom of the bank, though I'd seen no river on the day we visited, and the land around the church had been high desert. Life, the dream river whispered. Death. Closure. Summoned, I went. Irrational? I didn't care.

I remembered to take Nakai's CD. His Native American flute became the soundtrack for my solo pilgrimage to Chimayo, where I hoped to finally lay Lucinda to rest in the little church. In the room beside the pit, I left behind the pink cap my newborn daughter wore in preemie ICU, along with the hospital bracelet bearing her name. But when I got back to Ohio, my grief greeted me as if I'd never gone. It took a few more months to accept that, without my grief, I didn't know who I was. When Cass and Maddy showed up, I knew. Mentor, caretaker, counselor. I could pay penance forever, I thought, and be okay.

Returning slowly to the Pine Forest, I suck in my breath and keep my eyes closed. While my heart and hand continue to chord, the flute improvises a melody, at times low and intricate, murmuring like a creek, then booming like distant falls. Daybreak Vision, Turquoise World, Cleft in the Sky: Nakai's compositions had accompanied me all through the New Mexican desert, into the mountains, and back to I-70, where I finally gave up and played classic rock all the way back to Ohio.

Now the music emanating from somewhere among the pines isn't Navajo but Shawnee, the song of a native son telling the tale of knee-high corn, low rows of soybeans, robin and meadowlark, Maumee and Miami. Of white pines planted by Boy Scouts in the 1950s, never meant to remain alive this long, though here they stand surrounding our little group.

Everyone is looking around, meeting their fellows' eyes as if just awakening, gazing up to where the hawk still circles. Everything seems carved from marble, realer than real, still as Sunday sunrise. Mom is shielding her eyes with her hand and searching the sky. Does she see the hawk? Does she know what it is? Madison is glancing around, looking into the eyes of one, then the other, seeming to ask a question that needs answering right now. What the hell is happening?

Eyes closed, I fall through a crack in the earth into darkness. It feels like a cave but it's only the bathroom floor of the house I'd shared with my husband, where I wept alone in the dark after he passed out after drinking too much. Once again, here in my waking vision, something rises from the floor, enters me, takes possession of my organs and limbs. At the time, I thought it was the strength I'd called upon, enough to allow me to leave my dark womb and crawl into bed with my mate's face turned to the wall. But it wasn't strength. Like a straitjacket, it bound me, left me partly paralyzed, a barrier between me and any child for whom I tried to feel love. When I'd tuck in little Madison, kiss her goodnight and smooth her hair, I felt nothing. While I consciously said no, I'd accepted Aaron's blame. But the flute's, the earth's song says I can let go now, hand back the blame and befriend my traitor heart.

Abruptly the sound stops, and I'm back among pines and people. Though I wait, not daring to breathe, it does not begin again. The silence is profound. Where have the chittering squirrels and quarreling crows gone? I stare at my hands atop the guitar. Blue veins bulge, carrying the blood to the heart I'd thought too scarred after my baby's death to ever hear the earth sing again. But now I have. And everyone is looking at me. They think I arranged the flute concert as a prelude to the ceremony. So be it. My hands shake as I unharness my guitar, prop it against a tree, and turn toward them.

"Cassandra and Gregory," I say in a voice I hardly recognize as mine, "please approach the altar."

They do as they're told without hesitation, while the others gather close around the bower. I'm keeping my eyes away from Cassie's mom. I have no authority here beyond what these trees and the flute impart. But Greg and Cass can get the license signed tomorrow. What I'm doing is about something else. Will Mom get it?

I spread my arms.

"Friends, Father is not here. I guess a mother will have to do."

A nervous titter greets my speech. I notice, though, I didn't say failed mother. Glancing up, I see Madison staring right at me, eyes steely. Her lips form one silent syllable: Yes. I take Cassie's right hand and offer it to Greg, who accepts it gladly. With her left, she grasps her daughter's.

"If you have vows," I say, "now's the time."

They've been waiting, I know, for Father to lead them. Well, they'll just have to improvise, like the phantom flute player, like me. Hell, we're all just making it up as we go along, anyway. This ceremony, it occurs to me, is indigenous, rising right up out of the rusty soil we're standing on.

For a moment, nobody speaks, and I breathe slowly, in out. My own resurrection doesn't mean others are feeling the same thing, and I decide I'm all right with that. Then Cassie turns and beckons Mom. Three steps and the woman stands inside our inner circle, clutching her granddaughter's free hand. Mom looks alert and present, very present. Without further prompting, Cassie, grinning, faces her captain.

"Gregory Perkins"—a sidelong look at Madison—"I will love and protect and take care of you as long as I have breath, till the day I die." Glancing at her daughter, she murmurs, "You, too, honey."

There's an intake of breath so strong I hear the upper branches sigh.

"And you?" I turn to Greg.

His eyes, grave and patient, have never left his beloved's.

"Cassandra McCormick," he says, "I will do my best to love and protect you both. I'll strive every day to be the best man I can be."

He glances skyward then back. "There's a strength in this place," he continues, "that wants me to say something I thought I could never say, at least before all of you."

Oh God. I fear Greg's ego as I fear my own, that deluded monster that thought it could bury grief in a desert a thousand miles from home and keep on hiding its heart from itself forever. Greg smiles, easing the gravity inside our sanctuary.

"I'll be weak sometimes. I will need help." He turns and looks at the gathering. "I'll need all of you." When he faces me again, his eyes glow.

"Kate, we'll especially need your help."

What? Me, who's never been able to help herself? But when I see Cass and Maddy grinning at me full bore, leaning into the circle like sunflowers, I accept that maybe he's right. Remembering what we're doing here, I take a deep piney breath and say, "By the authority invested in me by this sacred place, these guests and you, my dear friends, I now pronounce you husband and wife."

While they embrace and kiss for a long time, we clap and cheer. When I steal a look at her, Mom dabs at her eyes with a tissue. She looks like she isn't going anywhere. The bed at the Peregrine just might get slept in after all.

Madison takes three steps and engulfs me in her arms. I clasp her back, smell her herbal shampoo, loosen one hand to stroke her golden curls.

My baby, my baby, someone is saying over and over. I realize it's me. My best friend's daughter is sobbing now. This child I helped raise with what heart remained after the death of my own is not letting go. Thank God.

Looking over her head, I watch the figure in the underbrush recede into shadow: a boy, naked from the waist up, with black braids, bearing his flute before him like a holy scepter.

Yvette Viets Flaten

Blackberry Harvest

"Ma," Ragna called, stopping her mangling. "Here comes Siggi."

Ma turned from pinning one of Pa's shirts to the line, her hand coming up to massage her shoulder, as she watched Sievert Hanson making his slow way up their drive. She had remarked once or twice of a crick in her shoulder this last week. Even this morning, kneading bread dough, she had favored it, Ragna thought. But Ma wasn't one to fuss, and she'd put the loaves to rise, and stoked the copper for this Monday wash, and slivered the soap into the boiling water without a hitch. But now, her face looked strained. But maybe she was just squinting because of the sun, watching Siggi.

It was a hot and close day. Pa and Albert and Oscar were in the west field, haying for all they were worth, because, Pa said, the weather was about to change and they needed to make this second cut of hay before any wet. Theodore was to do the milking, with Hilma and Andrea to help, before he came out to them. The girls didn't like helping in the barn, but were resigned. Pa gave the orders; there was no use to grumble.

Siggi, closer to his sixth year than his fifth, finally made it to the farmyard. He had collected on his walk a forked stick, a smooth stone or two, and a large, rusty colored feather that he was twirling between his stubby fingers. He came to the copper, where Ma was now paddling and prodding the present load of wash. He shifted from one foot to another, thinking, and then gathered himself up importantly, the hand with the feather coming up to shield his eyes from the sun's glare, looking like a dusty, pudgy, barefoot toy soldier, Ragna thought. Ma stopped her paddling.

"Good day, Mrs. Thune," Siggi began, using the manners that he was well-known for throughout the township, manners drilled into him by his upright mother and father who were known for keeping their manners formal, too, throughout their dealings with neighbors and at church, and in town. They had a good farm, with a big barn, and abundant milkers, and a reputation to protect in the valley.

Before Sievert got home, he would hide his treasures in his cache near the creek, wash his legs and feet well, and then get his socks and boots back on, to prove himself never so low as to go barefoot, as his mother warned him.

"My mother says that I'm to tell you that you are welcome to come over anytime. She says that you are welcome, and the blackberries are ready for picking."

"Blackberries! Oh, yes!" Ragna blurted out. "Blackberries!" She looked at her mother with a smile as wide as a half moon. But Ma was not smiling. Next to Yule, blackberry season was Ma's favorite time of the year, yet there was no happiness in her face.

Ragna knew why. It was a hard day for this to be the day for Mrs. Hanson's message for blackberrying. First, it was haying. Nothing was as important as haying, for without the good sweet hay out of the west field put up, they wouldn't be able to keep the cows through the winter . . . and then, what would they do for milk, and butter, and meat? Haying was everything.

And it was wash day. Nothing got in the way of Ma's Monday wash day, except maybe a funeral. Like always, the beans and salt pork were already on the back of the stove for tonight.

But today there was also bread baking, because haying meant hungry men, and a noonday meal brought out to the fields, so Tuesday's bread was set on Monday.

Ma passed a hand over her forehead and stepped away from the copper. "Tell your mother *takk, mange takk*—thanks, many thanks— and we'll walk over directly." Message delivered, Siggi began his wandering way down the drive, toward home.

Ragna looked at her mother. Her voice was not nearly as happy as it should be at the prospect of blackberries. Not for the prospect of the jam, and jelly, and pies to come.

"Ragna, fetch Hilma and Andrea. Be quick."

Ma gave them their orders; Hilma, the elder, was in charge of the baking. And the making of the dinner for the hayers, thick sandwiches of buttered bread and dry meat, and quart jars of spring water, for their thirst. Andrea was to finish the wash and hang it and load the wash basket with the dinner. Theodore, when he finished the barn chores, was to help them carry it to the field. Ma was stern in her words, sterner than most times.

Ragna ran to the chicken coop, where Ma's berry baskets hung. And she flew into the house for her straw hat, and Ma's wide brimmed one, too, because she knew this was a hot and close day, and blackberrying, while not work like her brothers' work in the hay field, was still hot and picky work. Important work, too, because nothing was better than a spoon of jam swirled into Ma's rice pudding come November. And Pa would say so, too, at the table, and praise his girls, who "braved the 'lion's teeth' up on Hanson's Hill."

Ragna would beam under Pa's praise, but she also knew that Pa's words were meant as much for Ma as her, or Hilma, or Andrea. And Ma would offer a second spoonful of the black jam to him, and he would sometimes take it in his mouth, right from her spoon, and murmur *søt, søt*—sweet, sweet—and Ma would smile, and Hilma and Andrea would look down at their plates, pink-cheeked, and her brothers wouldn't say anything, either, for a long time.

Hanson's Hill was a notable place; it was the highest point in the township, and the second or third highest in the county. It was on the Hanson farm, on their eighty closest to the Thune farm, rising like a cone from the little valley made by the flowing of Clear Creek, bubbling and pure, that Pa said was as "clear as a store-bought pane of glass."

It was a majestic hill, cloaked on the north and east sides by maples and oaks, and on the south and west by grasses and a few locust trees, some encroaching buckthorn, and bowers and bowers of blackberry brambles, criss-crossing themselves, and sending out runners to set new roots. And on this side, too, rising like the backs of stalking animals from the grasses and brambles, there were a dozen or so strewn boulders of granite, all cascading down from the huge round boulder that stood out on the very top point of the hill.

There were stories around the township that when the first settlers came into this country, the Indians would set up summer camp along the creek and have ceremonies at the top. One of the earliest plat books even named it Smoke Hill. But these days there were no Indians about, and the hill was on Hanson property, and the Hansons liked to have the notoriety of it and kept it up. They set great store in having a Midsummer fest up at the big boulder and invited the near neighbors, the Thunes, Mitnesses, Hoveys, and

Christiansens. There would be a cloth laid on the rock and all the ladies would bring their best dishes to pass. The men would talk crops and weather while the children ran from boulder to boulder, either as cowboys or soldiers or knights. At the tail end of dusk, Mr. Hanson would light a bonfire and there would be singing, and Mr. Hovey would play his Hardanger fiddle, and sometimes the grownups would dance a little around the fire. The young people watched the flames and each other, with shy glances, and wisps of smiles, and low words passed about. It was, next to church, the biggest social event of the year for the neighbors, rivalling even the Fourth of July in Cherrier.

Ragna loved Midsummer on Hanson's Hill, and although she didn't know exactly why it was so important to everyone, she had a notion that it was more than just a chance to play with Siggi, and the Christiansen girls, and Hovey's twin boys, on the grassy slopes. It was something more than that, more even than the ladies exchanging news, and greetings, and recipes, and advice on just about everything.

"Ragna," Ma called. "Fill a jar for us." And Ragna ran to the pump and worked the handle hard, soon bringing up a gusher of water, sparkling in the sunshine, and cold on her hands as she held the quart jar under it. She filled it to the brim and capped it.

Ma got up from the front porch step. She put on her hat, settled her berry basket on her arm and her garden rake on her shoulder. Ragna put the water jar in the best milk pail and picked up the other berry basket. They started for Hanson's Hill, going out the farmyard to the east, skirting the pasture, making their way toward Clear Creek. Tina, their old black and white dog, got up from the shadow of the barn and followed a little way, to the edge of the pasture, before she lay down, panting, watching them walk away. Rhina, one of her pups, had gone out at dawn with Pa and Albert and Oscar, and wouldn't leave the hayfield until they did.

When Ma and Ragna got to the creek, a swarm of dragonflies rose from the river grass along the bank and circled them, darting in and out. Surprised, Ragna yelped and recoiled, but Ma stood very still. "Shhhh," she warned. "They do not sting." Ragna tried her best to stand as still as Ma, who never flinched as a large glass-green dragonfly lit on her hat brim. Not one flinch, Ragna saw, and she tried to imitate her mother, but it was hard. Theodore's story of dragonflies sewing up little girl's mouths who talked too much had terrified her as a child, and it still left that image in her mind. Ma walked on, and the dragonfly rode on her hat, like a shiny brooch, all the way to the log bridge.

Pa cut a new log every spring, to add to the bridge, either to increase it, or to replace a log that might have failed over the winter. This summer there were four logs now, making for easier crossing. Ma went first, turning sideways, as she always did, and sidestepping across, holding her rake level, for balance. Ragna followed, careful to sidestep the same. Once, she had tried to go one foot at a time, balancing on a single log, like her brothers did, and she lost her balance and fell in. That day had been cold. Today, however, a slip into Clear Creek wouldn't be so bad.

On the far bank, Ma waited. "Ragna," she said, looking down at her daughter. "You know that we drink water from the well, not water from the creek? It's always best to drink well water."

"Ja, Mama,"

"And you know, if you have to drink creek water, you always take it from above where the cows drink?"

"Ja, Mama."

"Upstream. And if it's high summer, or slow running, you must boil it up. Or if it's muddied by rain, you let it filter out, and then boil it?"

"Ja." Ragna looked at her mother. She didn't know why she was telling her all this. She already knew all Ma's rules about drinking water. "Ma?" she asked suddenly. "Do you want a drink, now?"

Ma was frowning, watching the swirling water of Clear Creek passing under the log bridge. Slowly, her eyes lifted to Ragna.

"Ma?"

Ma nodded. "Ja, datter. Maybe a drink would be welcome."

Ragna lifted out the quart jar and upended the milk pail for her mother to sit upon. It was an unspoken gesture, and Ma lowered herself to the seat. She passed a hand across her forehead. Ragna unscrewed the quart jar and offered it to her mother.

Ma drank once and handed it back to Ragna. "You now, once. We must guard it for later. For the hottest time."

So like mother. Always watching. Always guarding. Always warning. And always right, Ragna thought. If Ma warned of something, it was best to pay attention. In the family, everyone knew that was so, even Pa. If Ma said to take a coat with you, by the end of the day, you would need to have your coat.

"Ragna, we go on, now." Ma rose. "To the picking."

The creek was on Thune property. The property line with the Hansons was five rods east of the creek bank, but there was no fence line between the two. Pa had simply piled five rocks beside the deer trail that came along the creek and then skirted up toward the hill. It was enough, Pa said, to mark their property, and Mr. Hanson knew where the boundary was. This puzzled Ragna, because all the other farms in the valley had fence wire strung along their property lines, but not them.

And it puzzled her too, that Mrs. Hanson always sent word, one way or another, about the blackberrying time, before she picked any herself, and that Ma always made a pie, first thing, but not for Pa. Last year, Ragna had asked her mother why she made a first pie straight away, and then walked it over to Hanson's herself. Not for Pa, but for the Hansons. And later, she would take over a jar of preserves, too.

"Blest be the tie that binds," Ma had said. It was the words of her favorite hymn.

And she had begun to sing it. "Blest be the tie that binds, our hearts in Christian love . . ."

And there was more that puzzled Ragna. As soon as their hay was put up, Albert and Oscar and Theodore would always go straight on to the Hansons, to help with their haying, which pleased her brothers because Mr. Hanson paid them in folding money and they had a lot of work because Mr. Hanson's hay fields were bigger. And her brothers seemed eager to go, too, because Mrs. Hanson was known for feeding their haying crews well, but then it was well known that it was easier for her to put on a big spread when she had four growing daughters to work in the kitchen, as well as a hired girl. Coming home, her brothers would take the short cut from the Hanson home, up over Hanson Hill, rather than walk the long way around by the road. And when they got to the creek, about where she and Ma were now, they'd dip into the water and clean themselves, and then come home, dead-tired but still full of spunk, as Pa put it, having seen all the wonders of the Hanson place. That's what puzzled Ragna; she tried to figure out what the wonders of Hanson's place might be, and she settled, finally, on Pa meaning the lightning rods that Mr. Hanson had bought for the corners of their mansard roof.

They were now at the foot of the hill, where it pitched up steeply from the valley floor, and they started up, climbing past the boulders that the young ones called Turtle, and Buffalo, and then past the twin boulders angling together to make a west-facing point they called the Pirate Ship. Under a nearby locust tree, Ragna set the milk pail and the water jar in the dappled shade.

They climbed a little higher yet, toward the Midsummer stone. Ma stopped, leaning on her rake. From there, they could see their little valley, and the course of Clear Creek as it wove its way through the green pasture, down toward the dirt road to Cherrier, the color of buckskin in the mid-morning sun. They could see their house roof and barn, and all the way, if Ragna squinted, their hayfield in the west. "Here," Ma said, surveying the brambles. "Look at this bounty. We will start here." She set her basket down. She reached out and chose a single blackberry and tasted it. She nodded to herself, then she looked at Ragna. "Take only the ripest. Leave the little ones to grow." She smiled at Ragna. "Like you, datter."

Ma was a good picker, quick and gentle, her agile fingers squeezing the ripe berry just enough to dislodge it, but not enough to bruise the fruit. The wide basket sat at her feet, and she picked handful after handful, dropping them easily down into it. Bit by bit, she worked around the bramble, moving the basket, moving along. Ragna did the same, although she was not as agile. From time to time, the barbs snagged her sleeve or her hand as she picked, and Ma would caution "gentle, gentle" under her breath, but never stopping her own rhythm.

After a time, Ma called out, "Ragna, take the rake," and Ragna, happy for the break, would reach up with it and catch the tallest part of the bramble with its tines and pull down. The trick was to pull strongly and steadily, bringing the bower lower to the picker without jerking it and dislodging the ripest fruit. One by one, Ma and Ragna picked the brambles of the best berries, leaving the tiny black buttons, or the unripe red nubs, on the vines, to grow. Bit by bit, they moved their way down the hill, their baskets beginning to fill up.

Suddenly, Ma stopped picking.

Ragna stopped, too.

Ma's hand came up to her throat. "I feel wrong," she said lowly, and she sank down into the grass.

Ragna ran to her side. "Ma, I'll fetch the water!" and she bolted down to the locust tree and back with the quart jar.

Ma's eyes were open but they didn't seem right. They were looking skyward.

"Ma! Ma! Here's water . . ." Ragna was fumbling with the cap.

Ma made a movement with her hand. "Make the pie," she whispered, barely audible under the lisp of the hot breeze in the grass and the hum of a nearby bee.

"Ma!"

". . . the Hanson . . . pie. Ragna, you. Promise."

"Mama?"

". . . promise me . . ."

Ma went still. Her lips were blue, from tasting the blackberries, Ragna thought, except now her whole face was blueing too, a chalky blue. It frightened Ragna. "Ma! Ma!" she called out and shook her mother's shoulder. But there was no word, no flutter of the eyes, no movement at all.

It shocked Ragna into a stone-like moment. The realization of what she was witnessing froze her for many seconds. Then she took Ma's hat from under her still head and laid it across her face. She could not leave her mother lying there, staring up into the hot noonday sun, alone, on the side of Hanson's Hill, without the shade of her hat to protect her, while she went for Pa.

Pa. A surge of electricity awakened Ragna. Pa! She turned down the hill and ran and ran and ran, weeping as she went, until she had no tears left, and her lungs ached to bursting.

Pa saw her coming first and stood up on the seat of the mower for a better look. Then he was down and running toward his daughter, his arms opening to catch her.

***

Ragna slid out of her bed and dressed in the bluing light before dawn. She had not slept at all, because, all night, she had seen before her closed eyes every moment of yesterday's events, every word, every sound, every movement. Even the twitch of the smallest piece of grass was etched into her thoughts, along with the larger things, her mother's still face, her flight across the creek to the hayfield, the shock on all their faces.

Ragna inched her way down the stairs, and out through the kitchen door. She did not look back into the parlor, where she knew a kerosene lamp was still burning beside her mother's body, even with dawn coming, and her father, sitting next to her, a statue in his chair.

Tina and Rhina were lying on the porch, and their tails waved once in recognition, but they did not rise to follow Ragna. On tiptoes, she went down the steps and then hurried across the yard, toward the pasture.

At the creek, Ragna stopped. Here, yesterday, Pa and Albert and Oscar and Theodore had not bothered with the bridge. They had plunged into the shallows, downstream, and then clambered up the far side, slipping and grabbing handfuls of the long grass to haul themselves up. Ragna and Hilma and Andrea had crossed at the bridge, so they reached Ma after the men.

Pa was on his knees, leaning over Ma, holding her hand. "No, no, Olina . . . no . . . no . . . no . . ." Albert and Oscar were without expression, like stumps. Hilma and Andrea were crying hard, arms about each other. Theodore had stood back a little, shaking, and, still more boy than man yet, had lost himself to an anger, turning and kicking Ma's berry basket with such force that his boot broke through the wicker and the blackberries flew everywhere. He'd wheeled on Ragna's basket, trampling it, and then ran off toward the south, great bellows of sudden grief rising out of him.

Pa and Albert had carried Ma's body down to the bridge and across the creek and home. Oscar brought the rake, and Hilma had carried Ma's hat. Andrea, sobbing, had linked arms with Ragna, but Ragna had no more emotion left. In her hands, she carried the quart jar.

Albert and Oscar fetched two barrels and boards into the parlor to make a hasty bier, and Albert said for Oscar to go find Theodore and bring him home. He put a chair beside Ma and told Pa to sit; he would go to Christiansen's with the news. He would see to the details, and Pa let him go, without a word. Mr. Christiansen, who worked wood, would make a coffin, as he did for all the neighbors. One of the Christiansen boys volunteered to ride their horse to Cherrier, to tell Pastor Wegge that he was needed, and Pastor Wegge would call Annie Mathiasson to come to Thune's to help with the laying out of Olina Stensethdatter, dead this day, the last day of August.

Ragna crossed the creek on the log bridge, balancing sideways, and she started up Hanson's Hill. Dawn was coming now, and she could see plainly the tracks in the grass where her father and brother had carried Ma's body home. She stifled a sob, wiping her nose and eyes against her sleeve. Yesterday—just yesterday—she and Ma had passed this way.

The milk pail stood at the foot of the locust tree, forgotten in the tumult. Now Ragna took it up and hiked uphill to the very spot where her mother had collapsed. She collected the remnants of the berry baskets and knelt and set them on the place where her mother had lain. Tears filled her eyes suddenly. "See, Mama," she said lowly, "I have come to keep our promise."

Ragna rose and walked to the nearest bramble and began picking.

William Bain

Fiesole

1.

There is a line of umbrella pines on the hillside he is staring at. At least a half dozen mature trunks—more even if he turns his head ever so slightly—driving their roots deep into the dry earth. Then the green needle-like leaves of course. And the grasses and underbrush up the hill and down along with the play of sunlight and shade. Through the spaces in the trees he can see brief patches of blue sky on the right; on the left, glimpses of the neighboring hilltop house, white, roofed in red tiles. He'd helped her out that time when she was a little short on the price of that sweater. London was their first long trip together. Staying with the hillside, he sees, between the last two pines on his right, an agave plant of some size. Just below that a patch of bright sunniness to the left of the final pine. The air. Silence. A wood dove calls. That is one of the areas where some pines were cut down, leaving big stumps maybe a half-meter high. The line of garage roof to his right slant-cuts off that sun-drenched zone, peaking on a line of cypress and Lombardy poplar, slanting back down to where the cars are nosed up against the concrete block planter or parterre, backed by the wall of the same material, topped by chain link fencing through which he sees more grasses on the hillside a dove call and lets his gaze a second dove answering go right back up the hill and stop on the pieces of white stucco wall, the red tile roof of the house, then settle on the middle of the hillside, saccade right, left. Pause. A magpie chatters. Fix on the pen point above his journal page. Dot. Silence. The air.

As the car door slams he looks up, then stands up. Peter, he says, holding out his hand. Giles, Peter says.

2.

The upper windows on that same side of the house also give onto the parked cars, the concrete block wall, and, at the top of the hill, the neighboring house, or at least what is visible of it through the trees, those white stucco walls, that roof of red tiles, the line of umbrella pines on the hillside seen from different perspectives. The mature trunks of the pines drive their roots deep also for an elevated observer. And the earth is dry. Very dry. The needle-like leaves of the pines, on closer inspection, can be distinguished by the way the sunlight falls, dividing the whorl of needles coming off the many small branches into lighter or darker green. The grasses, the underbrush springing up over the hill surface take in that same play of sunlight and shade. Then through the spaces in the trees, someone at an upstairs window (or from the roof) can see brief patches of blue sky on the right; on the left, glimpses rather like those Giles sees of the white house with its roof of red tiles, the dried root masses of some of the vegetation, the fencing, the walled material. But slowing down somewhat, it is worth noting that the hillside is covered with scree, distributed in varying pebble size, sometimes in different ranges of gullies, dividing the rich earth colors into different tones. Yellows. Red oranges. There between those last two pines, Clarissa sees from the left side of the window where she is standing, a big agave plant rising, the blue green of its leaves contrasting with their dark needles and the toned orange of the dry dead areas. At different points across the hillside the stems and open spikelets of the grasses whiten in the sunshine. Their legs had touched in the pool. *Nel mezzo cammin.* Her eyes fix just below that patch of bright sunniness to the right of the final pine on the right, one of those areas where some pines were cut down and the big stumps left rooted. The line of garage roof to her right opens to a wider view of that sun-drenched zone, and of the peaking line of cypress and Lombardy poplar. She can easily see the parked cars, their front bumpers against the concrete block planter with its backing wall of the same material, topped by chain link fencing. Moreover the view she has lets her see more grasses on the hillside as she lets her gaze go on up the hill past the fragmented view of white stucco wall and red tile roof of the neighboring house. Flowers, earth—below us in different senses. A magpie chatters. An invisible car door slams.

She watched the two men greet each other as Giles came away from the shade of the house and Peter came up the driveway to meet him. They were talking trees. In any case, she misses something they say when her phone rings. Is she anxious to go down to where the men are talking? For she does raise herself on tiptoe in an effort to keep them visible as she says, Well, whatever time suits you best, Elizabeth. And then, Yes. Yes. (Toeing it to the right side of the window to hear better as the two men move into the shade of the house, the back of Peter's head just visible.) Thank you, she says into the phone. Yes, teach a girl to fish, I'll say. All right (both men are now out of sight, blocked also by the right side of the window casing). Bye, she laughs. She then returns to the left side of the window and looks down. Well, what about that ash, then, Peter's voice comes through the open window. There is a silence. A wood dove's call. Silence. The air. Would you give me ten? Giles's voice. A protest from Peter. She laughed to herself. Giles: I think it's worth at least that. Clarissa leaned over the sill and looked out over the gray slate roof shingles. The dove called again. Silence. Air. Again the call. Look, Giles, we've (a second dove called; the first called back) always been family on things like this, but I can't really see ten. She silenced her phone, carefully placed it on the table beside the window. It was a drawing table, matte white, books and papers cluttering more than covering its surface. A friend had loaned them the table, later sold it to them. Without raising her feet from the floor, she edged closer to the window. Fifty-three Giles was now, two years her senior. Nearly thirty years now since that first trip to London. The top drawer of his desk was a medicine cabinet. They'd paid more for the drawing table than she liked to admit.

I could do four maybe.

It has to be more than that. I mean look at the tree.

I don't know.

I don't think you'll find one like that for less, Petey.

The last time I saw Paris . . . She listened.

Come down a little—four.

Four!

Five then, my last offer.

Peter moved out into the sunlight, turned on the concrete driveway. Like a military turn. He stood poker faced apparently keeping his eyes on Giles, who must have been some way back, on the concrete or on the tile walkway in the little niche in front of the door, in any case closer to the house. A magpie called and Giles's hand, wrist, and forearm shot out from beneath the angle of roof as a second magpie answered. Five, said Giles, the fingers of his right hand fully extended, thumb pointing skyward. Simply because you're near me. They'd bought that sweater together. When he needed cash for London she'd sent him a money order that Alma threw away. She knew she should go down and be polite. Should she change first?

3.

They had struck a deal, as she knew they would. Hadn't Peter found the house for them? Both men looked up as she opened the door and called out a cheery *cou cou* in the French manner. Well, Peter drawled, look at you, as she stepped across the red tile walkway and onto the concrete of the driveway, conscious of his gaze. They took each other's hands, left in right, right in left, as if about to dance, then exchanged pressed-cheek greetings. A wood dove called. I have just sold this man an ash sapling, Giles said, watching their little dance. Yes, I heard you two bickering, she laughed.

A silence. The air. Magpie chatter. So what have you been up to?

Oh, a few drawings, not much else, Peter drew his shoulders back (posture!).

Would you like to accompany us to the Accademia Gallery this afternoon?

Sure.

A bit of museum microcosm! she said. The roots of those big clumps of wild grasses on the hillside, she saw, were very dark, almost black. She said, It's one of my favorites.

You have so many favorites.

Ha ha. It's true.

Giles watched Peter remove his cap, run his forearm across his forehead. Well, isn't that part of what it's about? Anyway, she watched Peter replace/adjust (Giles had turned to stare at the hillside again) his cap those star shaped flowers, the dry earth and angled line I'm up for a visit if (Giles could see the shop assistant packaging the sweater as if it were yesterday) you lot Oh I'm all for it Peter said are.

What in the world was Giles staring at?

Have you made progress on that plan, she was saying to him.

I think so. Want Giles crossed to where he'd left to look? his notebook.

Clarissa and Peter followed him over to the shady area where he'd been sitting. She's wearing a dress, Giles thought. (So she *had* changed before going down!)

They looked at the notebook.

Peter said, For the fence?

Well, the wall. Like a boss. And he lifted his right hand as he spoke, then sent his left up and used both hands (at about chest height as I recall) to draw in the air (a magpie called) a rough circular pattern. Clarissa was nodding her head, leaning over the open notebook, looking up at Peter, who also looked and nodded. A magpie called. Silence. The air. An answering call. It's going to be lovely, Clarissa said, just the thing! Cement it on, Giles said.

Mary Lannon

They Teased Me About Him

They teased me about him—Lillianne and Lee—as girls will do. Women too when they are feeling girlish. Yes, they teased me about him, about Sal, our landlord.

With his narrow shoulders, conventional haircut and uncertain expression, Sal looked like Mr. Rogers. But, we always said, an Italian Mr. Rogers because he wore gold chains and favored a leather jacket not a blue sweater. We were all twenty-two, and at forty, he was ancient to us then.

Lillianne and Lee were my roommates. All of us small-town Catholic girls who had moved to the big city. Except we moved to the Bronx, not Manhattan, to go to Fordham, not Columbia, NYU, or the New School, the more desired destinations.

We were in our first year of graduate school, studying English, oddities to our families and friends back home. The $900 rent we split three ways was a good price in 1989 but still a small fortune, given our yearly $6,000 stipends.

Apple-cheeked and blond, Lillianne hailed from Wisconsin. The youngest of six, her father, a tile store manager. Her mother died when she a was baby. In her junior year at Notre Dame, she'd declared herself an atheist and a devotee of Anais Nin.

Spiky haired and defiant, Lee worshipped the Beats. Her hometown was in upstate New York, the snow belt a few hours north of Siena College, her alma mater. Her father, a police officer. Her mother, a part-time teacher's aide.

No doubt, they styled themselves romantic rebels, and maybe they were in their own small way.

Then there was me, Kathleen, (always called Kathy), the plainest of the three, with drab brown hair and an awkward manner. I had arrived from a small town in New Jersey, still surrounded by farms; my father, a mechanic; my mother, a homemaker. No romantic rebel, it was Charlotte Bronte's *Villette* that had inspired

me in my senior year at Rutgers to reject law school—to my parents'
intense dismay—and to become a professor. A practical alternative,
I thought, that would still please my parents but allow me to keep
reading and talking about my favorite books.

Yes, they teased me about Sal, said he liked me, said I had a thing
for him too. A fact I vehemently denied.

"You have got to be kidding," I said. And thought how could I,
a twenty-two-year-old, go out with someone who was forty, an old
guy? One who'd never even gone to school.

Besides, I did not approve of Sal, did not approve of—I
hesitated to even say it out loud—his racism.

It was, as I've said, 1989, and all of us unabashedly believed in
the simple power of words, that saying the right words could make
a better world. We carefully said "women" or "gals" instead of
"girls"; "African Americans" instead of "blacks"; and "people of
color" or "folks" to avoid what we considered to be all kinds of
more specific and difficult designations. The imperative to speak
correctly seemed to trump all other considerations. In another year
or two, our idealism would be mocked with the coining of the term
"political correctness." But that would be in a year or two.

So Sal's words to me that first day when I met him were all too
damning.

"Whites and Filipinos take care of a place," he told me, as he
showed me the large three-bedroom apartment near campus.

Lillianne and Lee—in brief, awkward phone calls set up through
the graduate housing office—had entrusted me to find us a place
because I lived closest to the Bronx.

I did not state my opposition to Sal's views, and I told myself
that my words would have been in vain. Still, I considered myself a
coward for not speaking out. But the apartment was close to
campus, well kept, and on top of all that, a bargain.

Three weeks later, as I drove to the apartment—my car loaded
with all my stuff—I still felt guilty that Lillianne, Lee, and I had
gotten our cheap apartment in a not entirely fair way. I surely didn't
see all the unfairnesses of the world back then.

"What color paint you girls want?" Sal asked us, as we moved our stuff in, piling boxes up in our respective rooms.

I was annoyed with the "girls," but let it go because I told myself I doubted Sal would understand my objections.

"What do you think of yellow? Or how bout peach?"

Polite and well trained, we told Sal any color would be fine.

"I want to give you girls what you like though," Sal said.

After more politeness, Lillianne finally said, "peach."

After Sal left, we all looked at each other with glee. Sal was, as my mother would say, a character.

Sal became a fixture in our lives and in our conversations that first semester. He worked nights at the bar he owned and could often be found around the neighborhood during the day. I'd see him when he was painting the fire hydrants in the neighborhood ("the city doesn't do it enough; I like to take care of a place"), or when he came over to fix the drip in the kitchen sink, or I'd run into him on my way to and from class or the grocery store. Always I ended up standing and chatting with him out on the sidewalk, the smell of baking Italian bread wafting over us. I was surprised that I enjoyed talking to him. How could I enjoy talking to a racist? What did that say about me? I did not dwell on these questions for many reasons but maybe chiefly because I wasn't that interested in the answers. Still, they nagged at me in quiet moments, of which there were not that many.

Sal did most of the talking, telling me about how the surrounding neighborhoods burned in the 70s because none of the "so-called minorities" took care of their apartments; how he was an altar boy at St. Rocco's when the neighborhood was all Italian. I doubted his account of history, but my own knowledge of that era was vague, and I promised myself that I would look it up, though it would be many years before I did that.

"They're all Albanians now," he said. "The Italians all moved out to Throggs Neck."

Another time when I mentioned my frustratingly small stipend, Sal told me he could get me a job as a waitress for gangsters. It surprised me that he used the word "gangsters." I thought he would say mafia, the term I was most familiar with. "Gangster" also seemed blunt, which, given the topic, I thought Sal shouldn't be.

"It can be a little dangerous," he added. "But they tip well."

For some reason, I pictured a basement room and me in a short black dress with a frilly apron, wearing heels and weaving among old scruffy Italian men. It would be something to talk about, and it would be more money, I thought. But I also felt that it would make me obliged to Sal, and I didn't want that. So I hesitated.

"There was only one time, I remember," Sal said, "that there was actually a shooting but nobody got hurt. It was just a scare tactic."

That scared me. I begged off, citing too much schoolwork. Later, I berated myself for my fear, sure I was missing out on a great adventure. I thought I'd bring it up again with Sal, but I never did.

"You'll never believe what Sal said today . . ." I would begin as Lillianne, Lee, and I crowded into our peach-colored kitchen.

Lillianne often cooked buttered noodles that she later washed down with dark German beer. She was the poorest of us—the least interested in cooking and the most concerned with good beer. Lee, who was usually on a diet, always ate a salad, favoring at first green iceberg lettuce and cherry tomatoes and later when she learned of its fashionableness—arugula. My dinner was usually pasta and Italian bread from the neighborhood. Like a tourist who wants to go to all the attractions, I was intent on getting the most that I could out of "the neighborhood" (words I delighted in saying).

Despite all the carbs, those were our salad days, as it is said, and the three of us dined out heartily on Sal stories. We told them in rounds of three at smoky bars to boys our own age, laughing.

"He likes Kathy best," Lee said.

"No, he doesn't," I said, indignantly. "He's just a sad, lonely guy who likes to talk to people."

"He's after you, Kathy," Lillianne said. "And you know what Anais Nin said, "Eroticism is one of the basic means of self-knowledge, as indispensable as poetry." Lillianne said this maxim often, provoking in me either the feeling that it was unlikely to be true or a sense of inadequacy.

Lillianne and I talked about going into "the city," as we learned to call Manhattan, to a museum or to see a musical or to go to a club. The costs and the stresses of grad school kept us mostly in the Bronx though at bars that looked a lot like the ones around Rutgers.

Laughing, Lillianne and Lee continued to tease me. But then sex was their favorite topic of conversation. They spoke of it in what I thought of as a nonchalant way as if it didn't matter. I was in awe of them. My only sexual experience had been with my college boyfriend, and I felt far from nonchalant about it. It confused me: Catholic school sex ed as well as the little information I'd picked up from friends and mainstream books and movies hadn't explained that pain and fumbling were part and parcel of the first sexual experience. So I felt sure that I should've just known what to do, and if I had, it would have been so much better.

I imagined Lillianne and Lee tripping in and out of bed, always in the throes of ecstasy, always wearing black negligees.

So I was surprised one day when Lillianne told me that Lee had never had an orgasm. She related this information in a matter-of-fact way, sitting on the former dorm couch we had taken out of the garbage. She had just drunk a couple of beers and was fast-forwarding through the commercials of a taped episode of *One Life to Live*, a soap opera she'd watched all her life with her sisters. My mother had forbidden such fare, which she considered trash.

"Nah, Lee's never had one," she said.

I wasn't sure I heard her right.

"Never had an orgasm?" I said.

"Never," Lillianne said and swigged her beer.

I wondered if she really meant never or just never with a boyfriend. For I had only recently managed orgasms on my own—though not with my ex. I did not share this information with Lillianne, thinking it a little too personal and wanting her to believe that I had more experience than I had. It seemed important then how much experience one did or did not have.

The term "hook up" had yet to make its way into our circles. So there was less ambiguity in the words back then. There was "going out," which meant sex in a committed relationship, and there were "one-night stands," which meant you went back to a guy's apartment and had sex and didn't expect anything more. We also knew that guys "jerked off," but there wasn't any term that I knew of for what girls did if they did anything at all.

So the girls or women, as I tried to call them, that I'd known—growing up—had gathered, talking about how you were caught because sometimes you just needed that physical release, so you just had to have a one-night stand or you might explode from unfulfilled desire.

When Lillianne told me about Lee's lack of satisfaction, I said, "Well, what's the point then?"

"It's the thrill," Lillianne said. "It's knowing you have them in your power."

I had no idea what she meant.

Somewhat embarrassed, I confessed that I wanted to fall in love.

"You just have to get over wanting the emotional connection and go for it," Lillianne said. "Men are right. Women take the whole thing all too seriously. Sex is a game." Lillianne expected me to be both amused and impressed. And I was.

Worry over final exams made us careless, and we forgot to put the December rent in the lockbox. I called Sal to apologize, and I told him that I'd bring the checks right away.

I walked the three blocks over: past the butcher's, past Egidio's and DiPietra's pastry shops and two blocks down passing Arturo's deli and Emilia's, one of the better Italian restaurants, to Sal's house. He invited me in to warm up, asked me if I wanted coffee. I hesitated, worried that I might be giving him the wrong idea, but it was way too cold to refuse, and I was curious. Sal's place was immaculate; the entryway had marbled floors and his living room, a leather couch, a big TV set, and a plush white rug.

This was odd. Bachelors, I thought, were by nature messy, as they had no wife or girlfriend to nag them to clean up. Sitting down on the leather sofa, I saw casually strewn on the coffee table a few *Playboys*. How could Sal have left them there with me in the room? Didn't he know better? It was all so strange. Men who kept a tidy house were not the type to look at *Playboys* or at least not boldly enough to leave them on their coffee tables. What if someone came by?

Sal brought the coffee. And the *Playboy*s just sat there; it was as if he didn't even notice them. He told me about Christmas in the neighborhood—how the gangsters paid for the decorations and put up a huge tree near the playground. All the while the *Playboy*s sat on the coffee table, and I felt both vaguely insulted by them and curious to know others' reactions to them. Still, I didn't dare ask him how women responded to the magazines (truthfully, I could only imagine horror from them and wanted to advise him that he might not be a forty-year-old bachelor if he removed the magazines). But I didn't say anything because that would mean that I had noticed, which seemed like the last thing I should do.

That night I told Lillianne and Lee about the *Playboy*s—one of the more tantalizing Sal stories.

We discussed what we might do if we were older and thus, perhaps, interested in Sal, and discovered the *Playboy*s, a magazine we considered low-class and tacky.

"Like that would be appealing," Lee said.

"Like, dream on, dude—it's all fake," Lillianne said.

"I just think it would be insulting," I said.

I almost didn't mention that Sal had invited us to come see his new bar. I had no intention of going. I thought it simply added to the pitiful portrait of Sal we had created. He was sooooo desperate that he asked girls half his age out.

But Lillianne and Lee wouldn't hear of it.

"Of course we're going"

"Kathy, he's your guy. You can't turn him down, now."

Once at the bar, Sal didn't disappoint. He wore a pinstripe suit, poured drinks, played Sinatra, refused our money, about which I felt guilty. Lillianne and Lee, both bigger drinkers than I, seemed to have no such qualms, as Sal repeatedly refilled their drinks, regaling us all with stories of "gangsters."

"You have to pay a fee to have this corner," he said. "It's like that in the whole neighborhood. The gangsters take a certain percentage. But it's the safest neighborhood in the city. No doubt about that."

Later after a few more drinks, Sal went on. "Word is that once a hit went down. And the body had only six bullets in it, but there were seven shooters. So the guys had to turn over their guns, and when it turned up that Frankie's bullet wasn't there, he had to prove that his gun had malfunctioned. Lucky for him, he could."

We were suitably impressed. Even Lillianne couldn't keep her eyes from shining.

"I'm on the edge of it, and I like it like that," Sal added with pride. "These guys know me: I was an altar boy with a lot of them. And you know I pay them their money and just do my own thing. They don't bother me."

We must have stayed until four in the morning. The last of Sal's customers had left long ago—only his buddy Al, a bald, fat guy who truly looked like a mobster along with Lillianne, Lee, and I remained. Sinatra sang on.

"I'll walk you girls, home," Sal said. "It's no time to be on the streets alone."

Drunk, I was annoyed at his protective "girls." Wondered what kind of protection Sal would really be if we were jumped.

Lillianne and Lee began to giggle.

"Kathy, you should walk with Salvatore," Lillianne said. "Lee and I will be in front of you, so we won't be able to see anything." They both giggled.

I could see that Sal looked at me out of the corner of his eye. He looked pained, embarrassed. But he did as they recommended. Right then, I knew that Sal was nicer than me or Lillianne and Lee or any of our friends. I wanted to prove them wrong, prove to them that Sal wasn't just a story to be told. I'll go home with him and sleep with him. That will show them, I thought. But I imagined walking away with Sal and feeling the burn of Lillianne and Lee's eyes on my back. And I couldn't do it.

Instead, I let them laugh and tried to talk to Sal about his restaurant. We said an awkward goodnight. His eyes still had that pained and awkward look that made me feel shame.

After that first semester, Lee dropped out of school. Lillianne and I couldn't find a roommate to replace her, so we moved out of Sal's place. He didn't hold it against us; in fact, he told me in one of our much less frequent chance meetings that he'd managed to extract higher rent from some male undergraduates who took our places.

Lillianne and I grew closer that next semester. She kept putting, as she said with glee, "notches on her bedpost" and trying to convert me to the practice. Though she excelled in her classes, she didn't return for the next year, deciding to work as a journalist for her hometown paper instead. Separated by hundreds of miles and immersed in our work, we promised to write but did so sporadically.

That summer after Lillianne left, I fell in love with Tom, now my husband. We met in 17th century literature, sitting in the back of the room, writing notes back and forth like high schoolers to keep ourselves awake in the hot room. That whole summer we only went out for pizza after class with our fellow grad students. It was only on the last night of the summer session that we finally shared a kiss.

I don't remember meeting Sal much after Tom and I started dating, but it might have been that I lingered less, as those days were always hurried, rushing to spend the little time I had with Tom and with his guidance, finally having decent sex and seeing the city. I know I saw Sal at least once more when he told me the undergraduate boys had been a bad idea: they'd trashed his nice new floors and even ruined his peach-colored walls. That he was going back to renting only to Filipina and white girls.

Tom was a fellow English major, a Shakespeare scholar—exactly the kind of man I thought I would marry. When we first met, Tom mistook my old clothes for trendy thrift shop purchases when, in fact, they were a result of few funds. He took me to the city, to the museums, to foreign films, to the theater and to galleries.

"How do you know where to go?" I asked him on one occasion. He explained that he read the *New Yorker* and the *Village Voice*, publications that I had never heard of (I'd read *Readers' Digest* and *Time* magazine my whole life) and the arts section of the *Times*, a newspaper that I had always considered snooty. Tom could cite not only his favorite bands and authors (as I called them then), but also his favorite directors and contemporary artists. I felt my sense of self crumbling. It was as if I was looking at the same sky, but it looked different: bluer and vaster and overwhelming. I clung to Tom, a steadying guide. The sex helped. It was an escape and a solace, for

Tom was a good lover, though it was never quite the ecstatic utopia I imagined in my innocence.

I also wondered how Tom could afford all our excursions on his stipend, though I was too shy to ask. Later, I found out that his parents sent him monthly checks to help as they considered him a starving student. My parents had tended to see me as an adult who should be responsible for her own decisions and her own livelihood.

Our marriage has worked for the most part. I'd envisioned us always reading by the fire with a few children by our sides. It isn't quite like that, of course. I don't need to cling so much anymore, as my sense of self and world has stabilized, but I suppose Tom misses the clinging. And Tom isn't quite the man I thought he was; his brilliance turned out to be a result of a more sophisticated education and is tinged with insecurity (whose isn't? I remind myself on trying days); he doesn't have as much of a sense of humor as I thought he had (a lot of our jokes had been on me, my naivete). There are topics that must be tiptoed over. But I am sure that I am not the woman that Tom thought he married either. We have adjusted, I think. And we have good kids: a thirteen-year-old boy and a nine-year-old girl, and Tom's a great father, if sometimes a bit overbearing. And we do make it a point to read by the fire.

It helps me to remind myself that my life is so full: my great kids, a great job with great students. Some of whom remind me of myself at their age, small town, white girls full of idealism. Political correctness stayed around, it seems, at least in some circles and is staging something of a comeback. I sometimes say to these students that there's so much more than getting the words right, and they say they know (and maybe they do), eyeing me suspiciously, unsure, I think, if I have the correct bonafides. After all, I am old, and so likely out of touch (and, of course, maybe I am).

Lillianne came to my wedding—scheduled after both Tom and I completed our comprehensive exams—and brought her fiancé Bob along, a beer-guzzling, football-watching Midwesterner with a wicked grin.

At the bachelorette party, Lilliane told me she had to tell me something. She didn't like to admit it, but Lee wasn't the only one who had been having lousy sex. She never realized it until Bob came along. She wanted to make sure everything was good with me and Tom; she offered to tell me what Bob did that worked so well. But I demurred.

I must admit that even then, when thanks to Tom, I was more worldly, her confession shocked me. I'd wanted sexual daredevils that knew no bounds, and even if I couldn't be one, I at least could listen to their stories, but they'd turned out to be teases, alluring stories, nothing more.

Bob would cheat on Lillianne days before their planned wedding, and Lillianne would later marry another red-headed Midwesterner, named Andy. She and I still send Christmas cards with pictures of our kids.

My fortieth birthday is just a few months away and I keep thinking of Sal—the only significant forty-year-old in my past, I guess. He must be almost 60 now, and even that doesn't seem so old anymore. But I know that it's the younger me that's my true interest: how little I knew of men or the world!

I can't help thinking about all the chances that I didn't take. If by living as I intended, I wonder, did I miss something important? I can't put my finger on it, but I feel it might be there underneath my refusals and my judgments. But aren't we our refusals and our judgments as much as we are our impulsive jumps and our acceptances of life? For that matter, aren't we the stories that we tell or can't tell, or the ones we want to believe? I'm not sure if I am alarmed or comforted by these questions. A bit of both, perhaps.

That long ago night at the bar, as we walked, Sal's shoes made an eerie echo as he took each step in the quiet. It was that time between the night and the early morning when the sky just begins to lighten. Out on the Bronx streets only the hardiest of late-night revelers were returning home. The bus drivers and garbage men had yet to begin their rounds. Sensible people had long since gone to bed. I am, it seems, one of those sensible people now.

James Callan

Phantoms

He used to stand outside the shower while I washed myself. He'd make funny faces at himself in the mirror and sometimes dance. More often than not, he'd ask me to draw pictures in the condensation that fogged up white on the glass partition. I'd scrawl a T-Rex with my finger. A tree. A happy face. A truck. So many trucks. His requests came one after the other. A fire engine. A police car. Cement mixer, street cleaner, double-trailer semi. In the end, I'd run out of space or I'd run out of hot water. The intended quick rinse would become a quarter-hour doodle.

I'd emerge from the shower, cleaner than I needed to be. Ten minutes cleaner. But his smiles and excitement have made every minute worth it. His beautiful face is imprinted on my mind, like a doodle scrawled in fog.

Sometimes he'd offer me the towel, which was cute on its own, but then he'd say, "Don't catch cold, Daddy," or, "I'll warm you up," and I'd practically melt. After a long shower the cramped bathroom would temporarily become the Amazon rainforest, the deepest reaches of the Congo. This was the last place anyone would catch cold. Dry enough, I'd wade the sweltering soup of spectral mist, my son's tiny hand in my own. Then it was story time. Then bed.

One time I drew my son a sailboat. A steamboat. A cruise ship. A canoe. I'd draw the horizontal crests of identical, repetitive waves. I drew a pirate ship with a crude skull and crossbones. I taught my boy all about the Jolly Roger. It was then he decided he wished to become a pirate. "Here's your towel, Daddy. Don't catch cold." I'd smile and laugh. Then he'd add a boisterous "Arrrgh!" which I supposed turned a loving gesture into an act of piracy. After all, he has stolen my heart.

Our backyard edges the banks of a lazy river, a meager offshoot of the Mississippi. Brown and mercurial, it crawls, apathetic, a mud-thick scion of far greater waters. Catfish twice the size of my toddler rest unseen among the cold clay. It was easy to turn them into dreaded sea monsters, the river itself into the vast, endless ocean. It was easy to transform a simple aluminum canoe into a black-sailed schooner. It was a simple thing to gaze at Jolly Roger rippling in the wind.

My son and I left port and rode a zephyr under swathes of black canvas. I paddled the thick, brown waters to take us out and something jumped to disturb the surface. My son shrieked and giggled. He shook his tiny fist and growled "Arrrgh." Bloated carp and ornery snapping turtles, leviathans and krakens. An old Coke can turned pale with age and sun, pirate treasure. Booty, I taught my son. Two intersecting logs on the opposite bank, the X that marks the spot. High adventure on the high sea. My little boy and I.

I've been a baseball fan my entire life but have never known the elation of victory. When it comes to the big game, a deep run to get there at all, I've only known defeat. I have only suffered great loss. My son doesn't show any interest, and that's okay. He is only four. It is difficult for him to understand how and why I insist on sailing back across the sea to return to our homeland and watch a ballgame. He cannot fathom why any buccaneer should wish to pass up the spoils of his brazen piracy, how any honest swashbuckler would ever choose to yield up both adventure and the plunder that comes with it. Tonight is the big game. This means nothing to my son. In our canoe, we play a big game.

He cries a little. Makes a bit of a fuss. He complains as I paddle back to the bank at the edge of our backyard. I muss his hair, golden, like pirate booty. It has never once been cut and shimmers in the low, evening light. I tell him I love him, and add an Arrrgh for good measure. He smiles up at me and Arrrghs in return. Together, we lower a black sail. We take down a Jolly Roger.

"Do we have to stop, Daddy?" His eyes are wet and hopeful. "Can't we raid just one more village?" I shake my head no, but promise tomorrow. As we walk to the house, I contemplate the chances my son would develop an interest in baseball if we moved to Pittsburgh where he could root for the Pirates. It is a ridiculous notion, moving halfway across the country for a mascot that might amuse a little kid. Yes, a ridiculous notion. The Pirates are terrible.

Inside, I cut my boy some carrots. I make him a sandwich and amputate the crusts with a cutlass. I leave a blob of jam on his plate for him to dip the removed crusts, a routine that has now become the expectation. I furnish my son with Legos, including the little pirate set. "Can we play pirates after the game, Daddy?" He smiles up at me from the carpet, a smear of raspberry jam across his cheek, a wound from a skirmish, a red tally left by an angry captain's hooked hand or the crude wooden spear of an island native. "We can sail under the cover of darkness! Can we, Daddy? Can we please?" Tomorrow, I say. I take the wind from his sails.

My team wins the game and at long last I know elation. No longer must I suffer great losses. This is my golden moment. This is what it feels like to be a champion. I have envisioned this for many years. I have played pretend in my mind. Reality is so much sharper, so much sweeter. Reality swoops down.

Way past his bedtime, I must hurry to put my boy to sleep. I call out to him and wonder if he has done it himself. Usually it's bedtime stories and a cuddle, then lights out. Often, it requires more. Sometimes I lay there in the dark and hold him until he drifts off. Sometimes he says I can go, but usually he says that he needs me. If he has put himself to bed I will be both proud and sad. Another milestone. The years fly by.

Beside the couch rests a plate with uneaten carrots, a blob of jam and four crusts. There is a tiny, U-shaped bite in his sandwich, but otherwise his dinner has gone uneaten. My boy is ravenous. Not a picky eater. I worry and rush to his bedroom. In my haste, I trample a small Lego set. I obliterate a pirate ship. I stumble and swear and rub my foot. When I get to my son's bedroom it is dark and empty. My cries echo, as if from a seaside grotto.

Out into the night, I drown in panic. I drown in my imagination, which is cold and dark and has no bottom. I do not drown in the river, but I drown in the reality that engulfs me. There is no canoe at the water's edge. There is no child. I swim out into black water and cry out, call out, pour myself out, tear myself open. I drown in sorrow. I drown in the deepest of grief. There is no child. He, too, has drowned.

A sleepless night will bring a morning that is the beginning of the end of any joy I may have known. Dawn will bring with it light and allow me to confirm my worst fears. It will illuminate the first page of a long, endless tome of lost love. A great hollow engorged with grief. Morning will bring the end of everything. It will bring the beginning of nothing. All that is left is me.

When I take a shower I search for smiles. I hope to catch a glimpse of an angel dancing in the mirror. I turn up the hot until the water sears my body. I am spotless, but I will never be clean. Water vapor fills the small room and transports me to a tropical rainforest. Images reveal themselves in the condensation on the glass partition. Scrawled in the mist, a T-Rex, a tree, a happy face, a truck. So many trucks. A skull and crossbones. The face of death. A Jolly Roger.

So many images before me. Like phantoms in the fog.

Alexa Dinu

Earl Grey

Hello! It is wonderful to see you again, especially in these different circumstances! You know me, I assure you, although the majority of people I visit greet me with a sigh of desperation and a tired gaze. Since I visit everyone that wanders this Earth, it is a lot of disappointment I encounter, but I try not to let it affect my responsibilities.

But never mind me, because today I am here to do something a little different and talk to you about one of my friends (as chance would have it, I do have one of those). Sierra is in her final year at the University of Edinburgh where she studies literature. She has a blue parakeet, she is allergic to gluten, and she works part-time in a small café, which is the same information she provides when introducing herself to anyone else. I have been visiting her for as long as she can remember and somehow she grew fond of me, even half-smiles when I arrive. The way she sees it, if I am present then she is not really alone—damn the artists and their twisting of reality—but I always argue that being alone and being lonely are two completely different things. That debate never ends quickly, so I let it go.

Our last encounter was not anything out of the ordinary, but our subject of discussion was. It was the middle of the night, around 3 a.m. which is arguably the best time of day to "crease and smooth over the fabric of destiny"—her words, not mine.

I walked into the living room and found Sierra sitting on the couch, elbows resting on her knees, head in hands, gazing at a single sentence written in an otherwise empty notebook. I slowly walked around the coffee table between her and the TV and took a seat on the opposite end of the couch. She never moved an inch, her eyes locked on that one sentence.

"Working on a new piece?" I asked, trying not to startle her in case she hadn't noticed I was there. I know her better than that, though, so I was not surprised when she calmly lifted her head straight ahead and put her fingertips against her mouth, hands together like in prayer.

"It's mocking me," she said after a short silence. "It's been mocking me for days." Sierra let out a sigh of desperation, but I was glad that, for once, I was not the cause of it.

"The sentence?" I asked.

"Yes," she replied instantly, in a tone that indicated the obviousness of it.

"All right, what does it say?"

"It's a stupid prompt from my stupid creative writing professor. It says, 'What does love mean?' in very tiny condescending letters," she replied, slightly more and more annoyed.

I leaned in over the table and looked at her scarce notebook, considering the words and the implication they carried. The question's meaning and the weight of all the possible answers were now resting in the air between us. "They are tiny, indeed, but I do not think letters can be condescending," I offered, trying for some humor.

"Now you're the condescending one," she said, looking at me for the first time since my arrival. Sierra is usually tired—of school, of work, of socializing; of waking up, of going to sleep, of living— but that night it seemed like she had not rested in weeks.

"Have you asked your roommates for an opinion? That usually helps."

"They're not home," she mumbled, avoiding my eyes.

"Ah, I see. Hence me being here."

"You would've been here either way, you know that."

It is true, I did know that. I see Sierra a few times a week, even more. It is usually the artists I visit most often, and it is them who always unknowingly put me in their work, but Sierra is one of those special people I come across once every hundred years who not only feels my presence but sees and hears my earthly form too. We have learnt to enjoy each other's company over time.

In that moment I did the only thing I could think of to help—I got up, walked to the kitchen, and turned on the electric kettle. While the water was heating up, I opened the cupboard above the stove and retrieved a tea bag which I then placed in the blue whale-shaped mug Sierra got from her father just days before I met her. We could not have been more different from one another—she was born in a small town north of Dublin, while I was born from Chaos, along with mankind and all the other concepts humans have created to survive the world that spat them out into existence with no warning whatsoever about what they would come to endure. I must say, while I have visited every person ever to walk the Earth, been by their side at their most vulnerable, and observed every detail that makes each an individual, none of these futile interactions has helped me understand the slightest of what it means to be so emotionally complex while hopelessly unaware of one's purpose. I, however, have never questioned the purpose I was born with—the sole purpose I was born for—which is to fill the void humans often find themselves latching on to: the empty chair at the table, the free spot on the sofa, the dark corner of a room, or even the small slivers of space in between oneself and the dozens of other people trying to reach the front row of a crowded concert. That way I can go ahead and say I am quite travelled.

In retrospect, the circumstances of our first encounter were not the most ideal. She was just a seven-year-old girl back then, surrounded by people who touched her shoulder apologetically and family members talking about what a great man her father had been. So many people around her, and yet I was the only one who she didn't look straight through. Ironic. Knowing Sierra as I do now, on the eve of her adulthood, it would have never been my choice for us to meet that way, but it is something beyond my control. I exist in multiple places at the same time, wherever and whenever my presence is required. I believe filling that void for people is what keeps them from feeling completely empty on the inside.

Have you remembered me yet, or do I really need to introduce myself? My name is something I've never said proudly . . . Latin even got its word for loneliness from me, and with a name like Solus, is anyone surprised by the disappointment surrounding the concept I represent?

So you see? We have met before.

I poured the hot water in the mouth of the whale (the very creatively crafted opening of the mug), fumbled around in the fridge for a moment and came back to the couch, where Sierra was staring out the window now with a slightly more exasperated expression than three minutes ago. I placed the tea on the table in front of her and leaned back into the cushions, while she slowly turned her head towards the mug and then to me.

"What's that?"

"Earl Grey with a splash of oat milk. It will help you."

She considered the tea for a second and turned her face back towards the window. The main street of the family neighborhood she lived in was buzzing with a heavy tranquility.

"I don't even like Earl Grey," a reply which was expected.

"I know you do not, but it will remind you of the time you were actually in love."

I tilted my head expectantly and she tilted hers back with an expression which told me how much she hates the fact that out of all living and not living things it was I who knew her best. "Now come on, pick the whale up, and let us talk about it. Inspiration will come along soon enough."

She considered the idea, glancing between me, the tea, and the question on the notebook. Finally, she picked up the mug and took a sip. She closed her eyes and I could see her frown with a slight nostalgia, but she quickly opened her eyes again and took a more determined posture.

"Okay. Let's talk about it. How can I write about love if I'm not in it?"

"I was hoping the tea might help with that."

"And how come it's so easy to write about heartbreak, but so hard to find any inspiration for any feeling remotely positive?" I was at a loss for words, I will admit, as I am not familiar with the impediments of being an artist, but I knew a reply was not needed in that moment. She was quiet for a minute or two, while she sipped her tea, most probably burning her tongue in the process. The next time she spoke, her voice was small, almost like she was ashamed, a feeling I knew for a fact Sierra was not familiar with.

"Thing is . . . I don't even think I know what being in love feels like . . ." She paused and let out a short humorless laugh: "Isn't that the saddest thing you've ever heard?"

"Well, seeing as I am who I am and I see what I see . . . no, not really."

"That was a rhetorical question."

Of course it was . . . I am, to this day, still trying to understand all of the contemporary social cues.

"Okay, how about you tell me what expectations you have of love?" to which Sierra replied with an eye-roll and another one of her charming snorts.

"How could I, when I'm constantly failing love's expectations of me?" which was just as dramatic as her eye-roll. I stared at her with my face set and eyes unblinking until I saw the defeat in her shoulders.

"I don't even know where to start . . ." she said.

"It doesn't have to be big, or philosophical. It can be anything, anywhere, anytime. Believe me."

She pondered over my words for a few seconds and then said: "Sometimes, at work, old couples come in and order coffee for each other. They always know how their significant other takes their coffee. I've always found it sweet."

"So . . . love is knowledge?"

"Y-yes, I believe so. To be loved is to be known in all the big 'what do you want to achieve in life' ways but also all the small 'what's your favorite flavor of Skittles' ways, you know?"

"No. Not really," I said, starting to realize how under-qualified I was for the question at hand. "I don't think I am capable of love, Sierra," I added, and while that was a truth I have grown to be accustomed to over the millennia, I couldn't help but notice it stung just a little. Sierra could have surely overlook the slight hesitation in my most recent statement, but instead she chose to try to open my eyes toward one of the most foreign concepts ever to be born into the world from mankind. She considered her next words for a couple of long minutes.

"It's when they eat the pickles you pull out of your burger or the olives you take off your pizza. And it's also when you share food and inside jokes," she said suddenly, after taking another sip of her Earl Grey, now a perfect temperature. "Or when you talk to each other for hours with ease, but also the silence that follows is the most comfortable thing in the world."

I thought of interrupting her multiple times during the moments that followed, but listening on wouldn't have hurt anyone, so I mirrored her by leaning forward slightly, putting my crossed legs underneath me and giving her my undivided attention.

"It's when they water your plants because you keep forgetting and you'd be devastated if your ivy were to die. Love is in that first kiss that sends an electric shock from your lips all the way down to your feet and back to your head, making you drunk with anticipation . . ." As she finished the sentence, her excitement went down, and slowly so did her expression. Oh.

"It's when you teach them how to dance to their favorite song that they just played for you for the first time. Or when you're studying, but they're tired so they nap on your bed while you work. The sun is setting and the light hits their face just right and it's the most peacefully-beautiful thing you've seen in a while." She was not smiling, and at that moment, interrupting her would not even be acknowledged. She stopped enough to sip her tea again and went on: "It's when you're complaining about your cramps and how the painkillers are useless, so they silently place their hand on your stomach." She sipped again. "Which reminds me, it's when their hands are always warm, but yours are cold as ice." Again.

"I think you are getting a little lost in your tea," I interrupted. An artist would call this a metaphor—she was not getting lost in her Earl Grey, you see, but in the memories it brought up. She stumbled, tripped and fell over her words a little as she tried to convince both me and herself of the absurdity of my implications.

"I knew how to help you. It worked," I offered, but I did not know if the inspiration my help created was worth the hurt in Sierra's eyes.

She gave me another one of her half-smiles, but avoided my gaze. "It's only been a year and I think I can count all the memories of him on one hand. How have I forgotten so much?"

"Maybe it wasn't love," I said, with an uncertainty I did not even try to hide.

"Then I have no idea what I'm even talking about." She sighed, crossing her arms in defeat. She had always been her worst critic. We both went quiet. Sierra and I often sit in silence when I visit, but it had never been as heavy as that one was.

"I wouldn't know, of course," I tried after a few minutes. "I have never met him." A realization I had never had before. This girl is my favorite human, and I had never met one of the most important people ever to pass through her life and leave a mark on her soul. I wondered why that was.

"Solus, you represent loneliness, right?" she blurted.

"I think we have established multiple times that I am the concept of Loneliness, yes."

"So . . . have you ever met Love?"

"Oh, I-I guess so. We call her Agra," I said, taken aback by such an unusual question.

"Whatever dead language you want to use is fine with me, as long as we're both talking about the concept of love," Sierra insisted.

"Me and Agra cross paths occasionally, but never for long. Whenever I see her appear, I start to do the exact opposite," I said matter-of-factly. In response, Sierra glanced at me briefly and slowly placed the mug of tea on the table, gazing at an invisible dot on the wall behind the TV. She untangled her legs and put them down on the floor, almost like she was trying to ground her thoughts to a reality she had noticed for the first time.

"Oh Solus . . ." She frowned again, more deeply this time. A tear slowly formed in the corner of her left eye, falling in her lap when she blinked. "Love is when you're not there."

The silence that followed was only broken by the rain that started to fall gradually louder onto the windows. Lightning struck and thunder boomed, destined to forever miss each other, much like me and love as it turned out.

"Maybe I don't have to feel love to fully understand it, you know?" I tried to sound comforting, but I did not know who I was trying to reassure.

"No, I don't know. We have established that I have no idea what I'm talking about."

"No, you have established that. Look around, Sierra, love is everywhere. It is in your friends and your family and quite literally in the air you breathe. You inhale the love and exhale it back into the world ten times over. People will always fall in and out of love with each other; I see it all the time, but it never leaves. Love is always there, you just have to be present enough to feel it, regardless if you will ever understand what it means or not," I said, panting slightly, but looking at the cold tea on the table and her blank expression, I was not sure what to make of my friend's feelings. After another moment I started to think of something to say to disregard my short speech, because if I didn't believe myself how was she going to?

To my surprise, the tears that were filling her eyes were accompanied by a satisfied smile. "It's when you fall by accident but choose to love on purpose." She placed her hand on my knee, but whether it was in thanks or in pity, I did not know. Sierra picked up her pen to start writing, and she did not stop until she fell asleep, which was, as always, my cue to finally leave.

As I walked away and dissolved into the next place where my presence was required, I replayed Sierra's words in the back of my consciousness.

It's late afternoon now, and Mary's dining room is busy with friends and family members who are chatting about the latest work promotion, which cousin is pregnant, and a great-aunt who is back in town after years of being abroad. Mary is sitting next to her fiancé, staring ahead with a blank expression when she is startled by the doorbell and drops her fork underneath the table. I am here for her. It is usually the family dinner parties I am invited to. As she bends down to retrieve her fork, her fiancé mindlessly puts his palm over the corner of the table. I tilt my head slightly and frown as a glimmer of light starts to take the form of a beautiful woman just behind Mary's shoulder, a figure I know too well but never see for more than a moment.

Mary sits back up and notices her fiancé's hand move away from the corner, and somehow there is no need for me anymore. I nod towards my estranged relative now smiling above the engaged couple and walk into the air towards my next destination.

Huh, I think. It's when you fall by accident, but choose to love on purpose.

Clint Margrave

Trash

Dustin must think trash takes itself out. That cans magically appear on the curb in front of our duplex each week. He probably doesn't remember when trashmen got out of the truck and emptied the cans by hand, not some guy with a long mechanical arm. He doesn't remember when nobody recycled and your stuff went in the same bins and you could litter out your car window, cups, cigarettes, whole ashtrays, because people still smoked and there was smog and nobody gave a shit.

Dustin separates his trash, washes each individual bottle, before dropping it in the recycling bin. He thinks he's saving the world and maybe he is. For all that, my neighbor forgets that a wall is not the only thing we share. When it's time to take everything out, he's nowhere to be found. Not that he would notice, distracted by whatever podcast he's listening to on how to be a better screenwriter, with pricy wireless earbuds protruding from his long red hair. Which means that every Tuesday night, I haul the cans to the end of the driveway—especially now that the Boomer's gone.

The Boomer lives in the apartment in back, above the garages. The last time I saw him was a month ago, right after the stay-at-home orders, and he was wearing one of those N95 masks only doctors and health workers are supposed to have. Nobody's seen him since.

"Do you think he's okay?" asks Mags. "His mail is piling up."

"Maybe he went to stay with his girlfriend," I say.

Before this pandemic crap, there was an incident I had to side with Dustin against the Boomer and our landlord, Lawrence. Lawrence said we could put a barbecue or picnic table or whatever we wanted next to a little grassy patch by the garages. Well, one night, Dustin parked his truck there because he had a dead battery and it was too late to call AAA and the next day was street sweeping. Both of us got an email from Lawrence threatening to tow whosever car it was. Without telling anyone, he'd rented the space to the Boomer for his girlfriend to park and the Boomer must've messaged him complaining.

That night, I knocked on Dustin's door in solidarity, all pissed off on his behalf, then helped him push his truck back out on the street before it got towed.

"Lawrence is trash," I said to Dustin, offering him a cigarette which he declined because younger people don't smoke.

"Trash" is a word that gets thrown around a lot these days. Everyone and everything is "trash." The cops are trash. People are trash. Your opinion is trash. It's a good word. I like it despite it being so in vogue. The choking agony of the Traaaa. The soft landing of the Shhhhh.

Dustin didn't get riled up. You'd have thought it had happened to me, the way I was yelling and shit, my arms flailing about. I'd been drinking a lot of wine. This was before the pandemic when everyone else started drinking a lot too. Dustin looked hurt, like he wanted to crawl into a fetal position rather than punch someone. He was entitled to park there, not because the landlord had lied to us, but because the world should be more inclusive.

Anyway.

I try to get the cans out Tuesday night so I don't have to do it on Wednesday morning. But this week, I thought I'd let Dustin take the reins, which, of course, he didn't. So, sure as shit, Wednesday morning, when I heard the first truck, I gave in and threw on some jeans, and ran outside.

Dustin didn't notice any of that. He sleeps late. We hear him and his wife Astral or Azalea or Aura or whatever her name is up at all hours, laughing, banging things around, watching old *Simpsons* episodes. Sometimes we hear them fucking as if they're in our living room. Usually, it's on Sunday, just after dinner, around 7 since Mags and I eat pretty early. I look at Mags sitting on her couch, me in my chair, and we roll our eyes. Sometimes it gives me ideas, but Mags never goes for it. Then I kinda feel like trash myself. So, I pour another glass of wine.

Now it's been four days since the garbage was collected and the cans still sit at the end of our driveway.

"Just go take them in," Mags says. "It's making me anxious."

"We're all in this together," I say. That's what the politicians and journalists and advertisements tell us.

It's the principle, I say to Mags. Or you could just call it getting old. Old people are another kind of trash. Nobody cares about old people. When this whole virus thing started, everyone was like, well, it mostly just kills old people. I mean, that's true of all death. If Vegas were to reopen and I could bet on that, I would. Anyway, I don't know if Mags and I are old, we're more middle. Midway down the driveway of life before the universe dumps us in a can for curbside pickup.

"If you talked to him," says Mags, "I'm sure he'd be fine. He probably has no idea."

Mags, like most wives, has always been the sensible one in the relationship.

"I mean," she says. "If you're actually looking for results, that is."

"Results," I say.

Results make you think of those trashy tests they're sticking up everybody's noses. Positive. Negative. Who wants results? Who wants to find out they've got some virus? Mags thinks I'm being a little ridiculous in the middle of a pandemic to be playing this game (which I've dubbed the *candemic*), but life goes on even in war zones. People still sit at cafes as the bombs drop. The trash gets taken out.

And in.

It's not like Mags heeds her own advice. Though she does get more results. Last week, she found Astral or Azalea or Aura or whatever her name is sitting in one of our plastic chairs in the backyard.

The one thing we like about our place is that patch of grass. Our little sanctuary. Thank God for that. Mags sits there and reads. Lawrence hasn't sent a gardener in weeks, so it's overgrown, but Mags likes it like that.

Lawrence hasn't cashed our rent check.

We do wonder what's happened to him.

Anyway, it's not that we cared about Dustin and his wife sitting in the backyard (though let's be honest, they hadn't been back there in two years), I mean, they have a right, we're not the cops, these are unusual circumstances, we are in a pandemic. We have to be cautious.

Just to make sure we checked with some of our friends and they all agreed.

"It takes at least seventy-two hours to disappear from the surface of plastic," I say to Mags. "You can't just sit in somebody else's chair during a pandemic."

Do they think they're immune? Do they think that they can sort out microscopic droplets like craft beer bottles in the recycling bin?

Astral or Azalea or Aura, or whatever her name is, is always a bit too bubbly. She's the clueless asymptomatic super spreader who's going to kill everybody. Whenever we see her she waves by moving her hand really fast like some goofy cartoon character. She's not thinking about transmitting a virus on a red plastic garden chair.

Mags's talk wasn't to talk at all, really, but to leave Clorox wipes by the chair, and it worked. The next day they brought out their own chairs and placed a table with a cute flower arrangement on it, right in the Boomer's parking space. I was impressed.

To be honest, just like for Mags, it makes me anxious leaving the empty cans out there for so many days. It feels irresponsible even though I don't know anyone on my block and they're not going to say anything.

"Do you think he got it?" says Mags.

"Got what?"

"The virus."

"Who?"

I'm not really listening. She points this out. She means the Boomer, I guess.

"He is at a higher risk age than us," I say.

I peek out the window to check on the trash.

Dustin's living room faces the street, so they know the cans are out there.

"I'm sure he's fine," I say.

We haven't talked to the Boomer much for the two years we've lived here. We keep to ourselves. Sort of.

"That guy was donning a mask before any of us."

Mags and I bought a bunch of our own masks, not as hardcore, but cloth ones, at the dry cleaners up the street. They were selling them for $5 a piece. I got black. I kinda looked Goth. We leave our shoes outside now. Disinfect our groceries. Carry Purell. Wash our hands sixty times a day. Take vitamins. Even bought an oximeter to make sure we're still breathing. But every day in the news, you hear stories about somebody who took all those precautions and still went down. It's like you can't do anything about it. Like life is a risk. Like people just wear out or break or get sick, and sooner or later, end up trash.

"It is kind of weird he wouldn't stop by to get his mail, don't you think?" says Mags. "What if he's in the hospital?"

There are packages by his door.

"Come to think of it," I say, "he did look kind of sickly. Maybe he's immunosuppressed."

"Do you think he's dead?" says Mags.

One day you take out the trash and the next day you are the trash.

Just then I spy Dustin from the window. He stands in front of the empty cans talking on his cell phone with that same monotone voice he used the night I helped him with his car. No inflections, no anger, no passion. No arms flailing about.

I watch him go back inside.

"Is he blind?" I say to Mags.

Then Dustin and his wife both come out. Astral or Azalea or Aura or whoever stands on the driveway giggling and holding a pink and white hula hoop as Dustin carries some individual bottles out which he dumps into the empty recycling bin.

"You're not gonna believe this," I tell Mags.

"What?" she says.

"Come look," I say, waving her over.

Mags puts her iPad down with whatever show she's watching on the couch and gets up and peeks out our window.

Dustin's wife slips the hula hoop around her waist and begins twirling. We see the smiles on their mask-less faces as they both laugh, the empty trashcans lurking in the background. For a moment, her body becomes its own distant planet, far, far, away and the spinning hula hoop a ring around it.

"Just go take them in," says Mags.

"Nope," I say.

Robert Pope

The Freezer

As I drove home that night it began to snow, the first snow of an Ohio winter, light but steady. In what could not have been a coincidence, Vivaldi's "Winter" played on the classical station. Angela said a first snow elicits reflection. You know what has passed, what is coming. What had passed was Angela, who yet fluttered through the common streets and alleyways of my dreams.

Because it had gotten dark so early, I suppose, I saw the lighted sign of a bar I had not noticed before: The Details. I pulled off the road into the parking lot and sat a few minutes to hear the end of the music. The snow had picked up enough that I had to shake it off my coat before I hung it on a hook along the entrance hallway. I did not expect the crowd, though it made sense, given it was a Friday in late November, the advent of seasonal celebrations. I went to the bar and had no trouble getting a beer from the beautiful dark-haired barmaid, but once I had it, I saw nowhere to sit.

A jazzy combo played on the stage, a fat man on the piano, a skinny one on the flute, and a tall, blonde woman singing a song with no words—none I could make out. I decided to down my beer and leave when I heard someone say, "Excuse me." When I looked for the source, I saw a man smiling from the only table that fit no more than two customers.

"Join me," he said, loud enough to be heard over the swirling voices. He looked forty, maybe a little older, dark complected, with a streak of gray in his hair and a goatee beard, no mustache. His dark shirt open at the collar, a gold watch on his wrist. He looked unusual but harmless, so I sat across from him.

"Obliged," I said. "Quite a crowd." I was speaking unusually loud for fear he wouldn't hear me, and I would have to repeat my banal comments.

He picked up his martini, finished it in a swallow, and twirled the stem between his fingers. "The name is Lucky," he said. He set the glass down and offered his hand across the table. "Lucky Jones." He had a bit of an English accent, to my ear.

"Jack O'Shea," I told him, giving his hand a quick shake. For lack of anything else to say, I asked, "What brings you out tonight?"

"Clearly, to meet you, my good man."

I chuckled at this. He reminded me a little of the actor James Mason, enough to amuse me more than he should have. "Then I'm glad that I have come," I said.

"As am I," he said, "since I own the joint."

"Ah," I said, "then I am honored to sit with you."

"And now it's my turn to ask what brings you in tonight?"

"The cold, the snow," I said. "I was coming home from work and saw the sign for the first time."

"It's snowing, then?"

"Yes, it is."

"Where do you work?"

"I'm a cook at Steaks N Burgers in Stow."

"Is that right?"

"Also finishing a graduate degree at the university."

"Oh, that's fine. What's your field of study?"

"I am in the Master of Fine Arts program, in fiction writing."

"Fiction, eh? What sort of fiction do you write?"

"I am finishing a novel for my thesis at the moment, called *The Freezer*. Mystery with a bit of horror along the way. Start one place, end up someplace else. That's the idea."

"Sounds cheery, doesn't it? Do you have a publisher?"

"I'd love to find one. The immediate goal is to complete the degree."

"Isn't that putting the cart before the horse?"

"How so?"

"How long have you worked on this novel of yours?"

"Going on three years."

"And how long is it?"

"I'm on Chapter Thirteen. Maybe three-hundred pages in."

"With all the work you've put in, I should think you'd be more concerned about getting it published than completing a degree. Economically speaking. It makes sense to get paid for your work."

He signaled to a passing waiter and ordered shots of Crown Royal, neat, wagging two fingers to indicate we should both get one.

"You wouldn't cook for free, would you?" he continued.

"Absolutely not."

"Why should you write for free?"

"I would be happy to get paid for writing."

"Of course, you would. That's out of the way, then. Now, why do you think you haven't seen the sign before?"

"Not certain. It's been getting dark earlier, and I saw the lights. Very effective."

He blinked, waiting for me to continue. By this time, the blonde woman was singing a song I vaguely recognized as "Clouds."

"My girlfriend has been gone two weeks. I had no reason to hurry home."

He blinked again.

"She left you?"

"She said she was getting too old to live on pipe dreams. She told me in a letter."

"In a letter, you say?"

And she sat there on our bed while I read it, in blue shirt, jeans, hiking boots, a packed suitcase beside her on the floor. Her blonde hair pulled back in a ponytail. Right about this time, when I got home from work. "Yes. That's correct."

"And, was she right?"

I sighed unexpectedly, and when I realized how that would look, I shrugged to cover it, and then, to complicate matters, I swallowed too loudly.

"She isn't old, by any means," I said.

"So, you stopped by to drown your sorrows?"

I shook my head. "I liked the name of your bar."

"The Details?"

"Yes. I've been thinking about the details I must go back and get in the early part of my novel, now that I know where it's going. I saw the sign."

"Is that all?"

I thought a moment before I revealed the final reason. "My main character has just stopped, at this point in the narrative, at a bar, and because I have been thinking about these details, I named the bar The Details."

"So, when you saw the sign for the first time, it gave you a jolt."

"Yes."

"That strikes me as a very literary reason to name your bar," he said.

"Not entirely."

"How so?"

"My main character is going to this actual bar in the hope of meeting the devil, as a way to solve all his problems, but keeps confusing this novel he's writing with reality. Always trying to make sense of details until he sees the face of the devil behind the fakes, laughing at him. I don't know if any of this makes sense."

He laughed gently. "No, I'm intrigued. I get your logic. The devil is in the details."

I blushed intensely. "That was pretty easy to figure out."

"Maybe not for everyone," he said. He gave me his most ingratiating smile. "After all, this is my bar, and perhaps I can be the devil in The Details."

"That had not occurred to me."

Our Crown Royal arrived, two generous shots. He told the waiter two more.

"It's not exactly honeydew and the milk of paradise," he said, "but it's what we have."

We clicked glasses and he slugged it back. I took it in three sips because it tasted so good. I set the empty on the oversized cocktail napkin with the words The Details and the partial outline of a face with a chin beard.

The blonde woman on the stage explained that she was taking a break, but the other two would remain. The sound they made was pleasant enough. Lucky Jones returned to our topic of conversation.

"So, it was fortuitous, our meeting here?"

Now I laughed nervously but happily. "I suppose so."

"Shall I make out a contract then? Get your signature in blood?"

"What are you promising?"

"The standard," he said. "What are you making at this Steak N Burger?"

"Twelve dollars an hour," I confessed. "I'm also teaching a composition course at the university, as a student assistant. That pays tuition and books."

"Horrifying," he said, and he laughed a little too high. "You're working as a cook and teacher and novelist and barely scraping by, am I right?"

"You are correct, my good man." I expected him to laugh again, but he did not.

"And your girlfriend evaporated into the atmosphere. So, I would suppose, were I the devil, I would promise you first that your novel would get published."

"Done!" I nearly shouted.

He held up his hand. "That's only enough if you're not taking me seriously. Let's say, I offer you a job here, as bartender, if you have those skills, with a promise of twenty dollars an hour with tips."

"I have bartended before. I would accept that."

"And, finally, the capper, you find yourself a new girlfriend."

Now I was laughing harder. The waiter arrived with two more oversized shots, two more oversized cocktail napkins, and before we clicked and drank again, Lucky Jones gave the signal to bring two more.

"So, what do you say, Jack O'Shea, to my offer?"

"Yes, on all counts."

"All right, then. We take them one at a time. First the job. We sign a contract for that to happen now, immediately. Down the road will come the novel and the girl if you can wait."

"I can wait."

"So, we have a deal?"

"Do we sign in blood?"

"Why not? As a lark."

He slid one of the cocktail napkins closer and took a pen from his shirt pocket and wrote, "I, Jack O'Shea, accept the offer of a job, the publication of my novel, and a girlfriend from Lucky Jones, proprietor, The Details, in exchange for my soul on fulfilment of the aforementioned promises."

When he slid it in front of me, I read it over and couldn't quite laugh. The hand was pinched, tiny and jagged, and beneath this a straight line with the date underneath. Lucky Jones watched me impassively, finally handing me his pen.

"What do you think of the price?"

"I like the phrase 'upon fulfilment of the aforementioned promises.'"

"Would you pay the workman before he completes the work?"

I nodded a long while, and then I leaned in and signed the cocktail napkin, joking that my problems were at an end.

"Indeed, they are," he said.

When I looked up at him again, he handed me a small pen knife he must have taken from his pocket while I signed my name.

"Prick your finger and place it anywhere on your signature."

I watched him a moment before taking the knife. The handle was iridescent pearl, and when I opened it, the blade thin and gleaming red in the light. I glanced back at the bar where the young woman served drinks, thinking what an agreeable change of employment this would be.

I stuck my finger and splotched it over my signature. There was more blood than expected, and I wrapped it in another napkin to staunch the flow. Lucky Jones reached across the table and took the contract between thumb and forefinger, waving it to dry the blood.

"Do you see that lovely girl behind the bar?" he said.

I turned and looked at her again. I had noticed her long dark hair and high cheekbones.

"I do," I said.

"That's who you'll be working with. Claire. She's glanced over a few times to look at you. She graduated from the university where you teach a few years ago and has been working here ever since." He smiled at me warmly and leaned toward me whispering, "She's been through a lot. There aren't many like her. She's under contract as well."

I looked around again and saw her watching. I felt my heartbeat in my chest and temples. The third shots arrived, and we sat back sipping. We clonked the bottoms on the table.

"Now," he said, "go home, get some sleep. Tomorrow morning, do some more work on that novel of yours. *The Freezer*. Call your Steak N Burger place and quit, as of immediately. Report here tomorrow at five post meridian. I'll be waiting with the pertinent employment documents, and Claire will let you in on our rituals."

I stood when he did. It seemed a long time since I sat down. I felt taller than I had then as well. He was several inches shorter than me, though he presented a confident frame.

"Thank you, sir," I said.

He shook my hand and held it a moment. "Glad to have you, Jack O'Shea," he said. He patted the back of my hand before letting it go. "Now, run along. You've got a lot to do."

I nodded again and left, putting on my coat just inside the door. When I stepped into the frigid night, huge snowflakes danced around me. I took the scraper from the trunk and brushed accumulated snow off the windows.

Sliding in behind the wheel, I realized I was high from whiskey. I sat watching windshield wipers flopping back and forth before I pulled out of the lot onto the road. The snow had a dizzying effect swirling into the headlights. I had a hard time knowing if I was back in the real world or inside a world of my own making.

At home, I sat in the car ten minutes, maybe more, forehead on the steering wheel. When I went in and stepped in the bathroom to splash water on my face, I saw the red mark on my forehead. Something else was wrong. The face in the mirror was Lucky Jones. When he started laughing, I leaned into him, jabbing my finger in his face.

"Fuck you," I shouted. "You haven't done me any good so far."

I remembered the evening I came home to find her waiting for me, sitting on the bed, packed and ready to go. She handed me the letter, her face somewhere beyond resolved into another world. I stood before her reading in silence, smelling like cooked meat. The more I thought about the situation, the angrier I got. I punched the mirror, creating yet another problem.

The mirror cracked where my fist hit, and I could see a thread of red. I checked the back of my hand. Sure enough, bleeding. I rinsed the blood off as well as I could, dabbed on the antibiotic cream, and wrapped it in a tattered but clean white sock from the rag bag—one of hers. I left the problem of the broken mirror for tomorrow, or the next day. It would do me good to look at it now and again. My knuckles hurt like fire.

I headed down the hall, more awake than I had been when I got home. I glanced in my bedroom as I passed by, and the sight of my unmade bed disgusted me. Angela floated in one corner of the room on feathery wings, waiting like a bird of prey. Which made me want to check the freezer—not a good idea. In the kitchen, my laptop sat on the white table, closed, her letter beside it, face up so I could see her childish, loopy handwriting.

I knew how much it hurt, but I read it again, and a third time as well, until I had myself in tears. I barely needed to read it anymore. The writing on the page spoke to me. Her voice filled my mind.

"Jack I can't live on pipe dreams. When I danced at Red Light you came in so often I knew you liked me. I thought you must have money the way you threw it at me. You were cute. You had big dreams. I liked the way you read your stories to me but when I said you should write a scary novel and get it published and make some money you got so angry it scared me. I realized how one-sided this had become but by that time I was living with you. Anyway here we are and you working at a burger shack and I'm not bringing in money now that I quit and all. How can you expect me to live like this? You work and write and go to school. You don't know I've done a few sets at Red's for spending money and I'm sorry all right? I don't like hurting you but maybe that's what you need to come out of this trance. This isn't easy for me. I kind of love you but not enough to keep doing this. I'm going back full time if Red will take me. At least he had my back and we had fun. I spent time with friends and laughed and had a good time. I haven't had a good time for a while now. This is over. I hope you know it too."

"You're leaving me?" I asked her.

"Yes." She looked determined.

"You think you're leaving me?"

"I am leaving you."

"You're not going anywhere," I said.

I tossed the letter aside. It fluttered to the table then lay down and went quiet. I opened my laptop, turned on the power, and made a pot of coffee. I knew I would not be able to sleep now, no matter how much booze I drank.

And, fade to black. The end.

What I realized much later was that I got in a couple of hours work on Chapter Thirteen. I drank half the pot of coffee and lost consciousness of time. Powering off, I noticed the bloody sock next to my laptop beside the face-down letter. I opened and closed my fist, which made a spot on my knuckles bleed a little. I ducked in the bathroom, glanced at my face in the broken mirror, washed the hand again, hit it with the antibiotic, and wrapped it in gauze.

I hadn't wanted to sleep in our bedroom since that last night together, so I usually flopped on the couch, turned on television, and drifted off as well as I could. But that night, I followed a stray impulse, going out to the garage, getting in the front seat of the car, and turning on the engine for heat and music. Waking a couple hours later in the early light of morning in my underwear, the radio still blasting, freezing to death, I tried to re-start the car, but an orange light came on with a soft, repeating ding to notify me I needed gas.

As I hugged myself against the cold, I noticed blood had come through the gauze wrapped around my knuckles and dried a reddish brown I call umber. That's when it hit me. If I wanted to write a scene in which someone froze to death, I needed to know what it felt like. I put the seat back a bit further and got ready to wait it out. After all, I told myself, it's nothing more than I deserve, and I couldn't think of any other way to get out of that contract.

Talk about bad luck. I ended up in the hospital with the kink that I remembered nothing of what happened the night I nearly died. Not until I came home and read my Chapter Thirteen. That's when it occurred to me I should definitely go down and check the white chest freezer in the basement. Since then, I've learned to expect that burst of arctic light when I lift the lid. There's a moment I see my silhouette leaning over the freezer to look inside from another angle, the perspective of another person watching me, like déjà vu in space instead of time. If you want to know the truth, that's what makes me twitch so bad.

Contributors & Their Inspiration

William Bain hails from Indianapolis, Indiana. He has travelled extensively in the USA and Europe, and in 1990 became a dual national citizen with the award of Spanish citizenship. Some recent publications include poems and a short theoretical piece in *Tusitala Project*; and poetry in *Wild Roof Café*, *Danse Macabre*, and *DeLuge Journal*. Some small format painting has been shown in collective exhibits in Barcelona. Mobile-inspired poems will appear in late 2022 on a third-party creative writing web application.

"One day I was sketching a section of Catalan hillside. A hot day, though I was seated in the shade. My drawing wasn't going well, so I started writing a description of the hillside in my notebook. Later, while processing description into story, ideas on characterization/focalization came in. As to setting, Catalonia and Tuscany have similar botanical geography, and notebook entries helped me set the story in Tuscan Fiesole, following spontaneous inspiration to expand. Additional narrative distancing then came by using historical names taken from some of Virginia Woolf's fiction—so to some extent 'Fiesole' is parody."

James Callan grew up in Minneapolis, Minnesota. He lives on the Kāpiti Coast, New Zealand on a small farm with his wife, Rachel, and his little boy, Finn. His writing has appeared or is forthcoming in *Bridge Eight*, *White Wall Review*, *Beyond Queer Words*, *Millennial Pulp Magazine* and elsewhere.

"I have a five-year-old son, Finn, who is my entire world. At the time I wrote 'Phantoms,' he would accompany me in the bathroom while I took my nightly shower, and just like in my story, I would draw pictures in the condensation, much to Finn's delight. Also during this time, I was very drawn to writing stories that evoked sorrow and grief, the greatest of pain. Why? Gosh, I'm not sure! I guess that from a reader's point of view, I enjoy being moved, sometimes painfully so. I think there is value to be taken from feeling the uncomfortable or tender emotions of stories, even if only fiction—perhaps especially fiction—as it allows us, as human beings, to relate to each other, to tap into empathy and solidarity that binds us all together. For the record, my son is alive and well. 'Phantoms' is a story, completely fiction, which I guess you could say was inspired from my darkest of nightmares."

Ed Davis has immersed himself in writing and contemplative practices since retiring from college teaching. *Time of the Light*, a poetry collection, was released by Main Street Rag Press in 2013. His latest novel, *The Psalms of Israel Jones* (West Virginia University Press 2014), won the Hackney Award for an unpublished novel in 2010. Many of his stories, essays, and poems have appeared in anthologies and journals such as *Leaping Clear*, *Slippery Elm*, *Hawaii Pacific Review*, and *Bacopa Literary Review*. He lives with his wife in the bucolic village of Yellow Springs, Ohio.

"At first I'd thought the story's major conflict would be between the bride and her mother, but the story steered me instead toward the wedding singer's grief. Since a mysterious Native American-looking boy is at the heart of a series of interconnected stories I'm writing (of which this is one), it seemed natural that he'd play an important supporting role. Setting the story in a place I know so well allowed me to focus intensely on character, conflict and drama, which seemed to develop organically. It was a lot of fun to write. (My two friends are still married, by the way.)"

Alexa Dinu is a 20-year-old Media & Culture student at the University of Amsterdam. "I was born and raised in Romania until I moved to the Netherlands at age 19. I have a part-time job in a small café in the center of Amsterdam, and when I am not at school or at work, I am just trying to navigate adulthood without being too overwhelmed by the myriad of societal demands."

"Although I was rarely alone, I had never felt more lonely than in the year prior to writing this piece. The process of writing 'Earl Grey' was bittersweet, because it helped me remember a time when I was a stranger to loneliness and made me question if I will ever see such a time again. I have sampled motifs from my own life in this story, but I added new details along the way too. Maybe it's a love letter I should have burned, but it's also a story that helped me find closure, about a character that embodied my closest friend."

 Yvette Viets Flaten writes award-winning poetry and fiction. Her early years as a military dependent gave her the chance to travel and study languages and history. Yvette makes it a point to write every day, often finding inspiration in the most common and mundane moments of life.

"'Blackberry Harvest' is one of several stories that grow out of my Midwestern Norwegian immigrant heritage in which history, family stories, and observation all cross-pollinate and flourish. The precise spark for this story comes from an afternoon my mother-in-law, Edith (also of Norwegian and Swedish heritage), and I picked blackberries on a hot August sidehill in rural Wisconsin, having been invited to 'come over' by a neighboring farm wife. Immediately upon returning home, Edie set about making pie; the first one baked was put aside for the neighbor, no question asked, no explanation given. I realized I was glimpsing an old tradition of community, sharing, and friendship that was still very much alive. I had the story's foundation then, and once I began, the details came easily: Images of old-time haying crews and farm boys I've seen, dragonflies swarming, the shock of sudden death, and how the young girl, Ragna, has to make sense of it all."

 Jennifer Schomburg Kanke lives in Florida, where she edits confidential documents. Her work has recently appeared or is forthcoming in *New Ohio Review, Massachusetts Review, Shenandoah* and *Salamander*. Her zine about her experiences undergoing chemotherapy for ovarian cancer, *Fine, Considering*, is available from Rinky Dink Press. She serves as a reader for *The Dodge*.

"'A String of Beads' took a long and circuitous path into being. I had been trying for years to write a poem that captured the feeling of guilt and regret that came with my memory of taking mussels from Lake Erie. It was the first time I had those particular feelings, and even at 47, I'm still a little haunted by the realization that my own needs could harm someone else. I finally understood the reason the poem wasn't working was because I needed more space to explore. It was a complex issue and it wanted to spread itself out a bit more than a poem was allowing."

 Sarah Kontopoulos is a Seattle writer born in Canada to Greek and English parents. Her work has appeared in *TulipTree Review*: Spring 2022 Wild Women, and *Big Bend Literary Magazine*. Her husband, Volker, and two daughters support and cheer her on in life and in writing. Her pet rabbits don't care and would like some apple now, please.

"A family trip to Crete in June 2022 was my initial inspiration for 'Happiness on the Beach.' It was our first overseas destination after the restrictive COVID lockdown months, and I felt so lucky to be there. Great travel makes us feel changed for the better when we return home. After I started writing this story, with Crete as the setting, it took me in the opposite direction. That is, exploring how tragedy during travel can turn everything upside down."

Mary Lannon is the recipient of a 2020 Queens Council on the Arts New Work Grant, a 2021 City Artist Corps. Grant and a finalist in the *Iron Horse Literary Review* Trifecta Contest for the long short story. Her work has been published at *Story*, *New World Writing*, *The Woven Tale Press*, and *The Write Launch*. Her unpublished novel, *Tide Girl*, was named a finalist for the PEN/Bellwether Prize for Socially Engaged Fiction. She lives in Queens.

"In graduate school, I wanted to try writing a realistic story, so I drew on my experience of living in the Little Italy section of the Bronx in the 90s. I had the beginning of the story for a long time, without knowing the middle or the end. I knew I was exploring attitudes about class, race, and gender drawn from the roommates, landlords, and friends of that time. One of my struggles was grappling with my flawed characters' perspectives on race. It wasn't really until the discussions of being 'woke' in present times that I figured out that I needed the story to leap in time. In that way, the main (still flawed) character could offer her perspective on her earlier attitudes and the events of her life. And so I found my ending."

Clint Margrave is the author of the novel *Lying Bastard* (Run Amok Books, 2020), and the poetry collections, *Salute the Wreckage*, *The Early Death of Men*, and *Visitor*, all from NYQ Books. His work has appeared in *The Threepenny Review*, *Rattle*, *The Moth*, *Ambit*, and *Los Angeles Review of Books*, among others. He lives in Los Angeles, CA.

"This is a work of fiction and any resemblance to persons living or dead is entirely coincidental, or okay, maybe not entirely: It was May 2020. There was a pandemic. There was a lockdown. There were neighbors. And there was a standoff."

 Robert Pope has published many stories in journals and anthologies and three collections of short fiction, the most recent *Not a Jot or a Tittle* (2022).

"The idea for 'The Freezer' came from thinking about the difficult lives and aspirations of MFA students in a graduate fiction workshop I taught at a university forty-five minutes from home—except in snow. I wrote the basic story when I got back from a long journey home one winter evening, backed off and looked at it over the next week or two. When I realized what I needed to add, what to take away, I finished a second full draft and gave it a new title. This happened again in a third layer, complete with rewriting and polishing at each stage. Weeks passed, and when I knew the story would be called 'The Freezer,' I stopped, as satisfied as I would ever be. I knew most of the workshop members would never give a moment's thought to a deal with the devil; but one or two, I wasn't so sure."

About the Editor

John Bullock is English and has an MFA in fiction writing from the University of Virginia. His stories have appeared in the *Antioch Review, Fifth Wednesday*, the *Laurel Review, Prague Review, Clackamas Literary Review*, the anthology *Open Windows III*, and other journals. He teaches high school English in rural Ohio. *Mark Small: This is Your Life* is his first novel.

Sheila-Na-Gig Editions